The Legend
of
John Dougan

A Novel

by

Robert Pollock

Eagleye Books Int'l
Walnut Creek, California

Eagleye Books International
P. O. Box 4550
Walnut Creek, CA 94596 USA

The Legend of John Dougan

Printed in the United States of America.

Library of Congress Cataloging in Publication Data

Pollock, Robert
      The Legend of John Dougan

I. Title

Library of Congress Catalog Number: 90-82882

ISBN: 0-924025-02-6

Other books by Robert Pollock:

THE PERSUADER
LOOPHOLE
SOCCER FOR JUNIORS

ACKNOWLEDGMENTS

Although a novel is generally the work of one person others are involved in its production. This is certainly the case here and I am happy to acknowledge the contributions of the following people:

My publisher, Arne Collen not only for taking the chance that all dedicated publishers must take, but also for his idea that the work be illustrated. For some reason this had not occurred to me, although I had always had access to the photographs and illustrations used in the book.

To "Q" Stone for her cover design concepts and illustrations, to Inge Behrens for her artistry, Trans-Pacific for their printing and binding expertise, Sora Counts for some splendid editing, John Collen for his work on the word processing, and Richard Baker and Clayton Headley for their photographic prowess.

Finally, a debt of thanks to Father Manuel Simas for reading the first draft of the manuscript and for giving me his very supportive theological views and generous approbation.

ILLUSTRATIONS

John Dougan as a Young Man	28
The Bank of Campbell	33
Mrs. Daisy McDonald	34
The Colonel	35
John Dougan with His New Bride Cathy	68
Cathy's Brother Samuel	71
The Trans-Continental Bicycle Tour	83
A. P. A. Meeting Tonight	109
Klaus	123
Five Hearses in Line	130
The McDonald House and Barn	132
The Bodies	135
On the Bed, the Dead Form	136
The Covered Body of Nurse Hisler	137
The Cabin	138
Sheriff Ballou and Sheriff Lyndon	146
Seth Churchhill, an Old Time Scout	149
Murder! Ten Thousand Dollars Reward	152
The Rural Free Mail Delivery	154
John Dougan, Fugitive	167
Identification	175
The Campbell Depot	190

CONTENTS

Preface   17

Prologue   21

Part 1. The Start Of It   25

Part 2. The Murders   107

Part 3. The Chase   141

Part 4. Twelve Years Later   163

Epilogue   209

And So The Legend Began   215

There is nothing stronger

than human prejudice.

Wendell Phillips, 1852

Sometimes you should do something for yourself.

This one is for me.

Robert Pollock, 1990

PREFACE

The original handwritten papers, photographs and illustrations that comprise the tale that follows here were discovered, shortly after his death, among the personal effects of a client of ours. He was not, by profession, a writer nor even a journalist, but it seemed to us that he had put down a remarkable story; one he claimed was true.

Investigation appeared to substantiate such a claim and for their assistance we have to thank the *San Jose Mercury News* and the California State Library for allowing lengthy searching of their files.

You will find powerful emotions recorded in these pages, and at times horrific events. Yet in all a tender, tortured story. A story that in spite of the time in which it took place, the late 1800s, has its parallel in many ways today, for love and hate are indeed two sides of the same coin. Or at least that has been our experience.

Adam & Benjamin
Attorneys-at-law
San Francisco, California

I was a very young man when this story began. I knew, or came to know, nearly everyone concerned in it. So, if I write about what the people thought and did in private you might accept that even though I was not privy to all their thoughts and doings that my rendering is a very close approximation of what was.

Although, I have to say, where the occasion warranted it, that I did make some literary presumptions.

I shall not intrude into the narrative myself, even though I am part of it, for I have no ambitions to become known, only to faithfully record a first hand account of the truth about an emerging Northern Californian farming area.

The photographs that illustrate this rendering were, in the most, taken from the local newspapers. Others, though, have never been published. I won't say how I came about them, sufficient to record they were, at one time, in the hands of the local sheriff.

We are in modern times now, of course, and that there have been tremendous changes goes without saying. But, I tend to think the changes are in things and not people.

Anon.

The Legend
of
John Dougan

PROLOGUE

PROLOGUE

Oak Hill Cemetery, San Jose, California, 1960.

Heavy gray clouds lay low in the sky above the deserted cemetery and the cold wind blew wet leaves across the cracked surface of the lonely, sunken family plot. Spots of rain fell on the thick-set figure of a man kneeling by the gravestones. He pulled his topcoat tighter about himself.

The man brushed the soggy debris from the face of the dull, weathered gray stones. There were five bodies buried under them and all had died on the same day, May 26, 1896. There was carved into the gravestones a series of words, one or two to each stone, under the names and dates of birth.

The man struggled to his feet and moved back from the graves so that he could read the words in order, left to right:

VENGEANCE... IS MINE... I WILL REPAY...
SAITH... THE LORD.

LEGEND OF JOHN DOUGAN

Part 1.

THE START OF IT

Campbell Station, California

The Late 1800s

THE LEGEND OF JOHN DOUGAN

THE START OF IT

Cathy Hanson first saw John Dougan in high school when she was fourteen. He was in his senior year and almost full grown, it looked. Tall, at least six feet, and slim, but with wide shoulders. His face already had the signs of being rugged like you would see on an outdoors man.

He was quiet, studious even, and always on wheels, some kind of bicycle or other riding over the dusty roads around San Jose.

She never got enough courage that year to talk to him, just to look. A couple of times she fancied he noticed her and that was about it until a few years later.

By twenty-one she had grown into a pretty young woman.

Slim, with a good head of soft blonde hair that became lighter and lighter as the California sun bleached it through the summer and early autumn months. She had an attractive figure and she turned more than a few heads every Sunday morning at the Campbell Methodist Church where she went with her family.

In the meanwhile, John Dougan had moved out of the area, north to Chico where he first labored, and then after becoming friendly with a local man he would drink with, he became a partner with him in a tree nursery.

He worked hard at the nursery and well, and his partner agreed that Dougan could send for his brother George to join him.

John Dougan as a Young Man
*His face already had the signs of being rugged like
you would see on an outdoors man.*

For a year or two everything went well for the brothers. Then a letter came from their priest in San Jose. Their younger sister, Jane, had become ill and needed them. So the brothers left Chico for home. At first they only meant to visit, but what they had thought to be a short stay grew into weeks as their sister's condition deteriorated.

It was a bad situation. Their mother had died three years previously after a long and painful illness, and their father had long gone - - gold prospecting, they'd been told. The reason wasn't important, he had run out on his family which had halted any ambitions John had about going to college. So at least one of the brothers would have to stay in San Jose to look after their sister.

They worried over their responsibility to Jane and their concern for the business in Chico. In the end they decided that John should go back up and try to sell out his share to Laxton, the senior partner and original owner of the nursery.

It was a reasonable idea but it did not work out that way. When Dougan got back to Chico he found that Laxton had himself sold out.

"Gone to Nevada," the new owner said. "Gave him a good price. Didn't say nothing about no partner."

The new man showed Dougan the papers and right enough there was no notation of any partner. Just an outright bill of sale - - one man to another.

John Dougan brooded about the deception but he did nothing. What could he do anyway, track the man to Nevada? He had no papers himself; the partnership had been a shake of the hand. Well, that taught him a lesson, he thought. You don't ever trust the shake of the hand again. Seems like there wasn't too much trust in his young life. Something he would have to learn how to live with, he figured.

It was a bitter John Dougan who returned to San Jose.

🍎 🍎 🍎

In the months that followed, the Dougan brothers settled into a new routine. George took up book-keeping classes to help with the job he had taken as assistant bookkeeper with a Mr. H. L. Miller, pro-prietor of a paper house on South Second Street in San Jose. John stayed with the land and began again as a laborer. Between them, they organized the care of their sister, whose condition had stabilized, although it left her more or less an invalid.

John Dougan took well to working the land. It was good there and the climate kind for most of the time. In the whole of Santa Clara County there were over 20,000 acres of fruit trees and 15,000 acres of vines.

Slowly, and in a modest way, the brothers began to prosper, and they took on the services of a companion for their sister which gave them more time to them-selves.

John Dougan used most of his free time wheeling and on weekends he would pack food and drink and head east for the foothills of Mount Hamilton. He always traveled alone and would sleep out on warm nights. He enjoyed the terrain and the hard going of traversing it on a bicycle. His body became hard and his knowledge of the geography increased with every trip so that soon he was like a mountain man himself - - a mountain man on a bicycle.

It was on one of these trips, while he was sitting over a small campfire looking out into the warm, dark night, that he decided he should take up a profession. At school he had been good at arithmetic and accounting, so he had qualifications, qualifications he wasn't using. He had heard they were opening a new bank in Campbell Station; maybe he would apply for a job there. It would put his talents to good use.

Which was how, at the age of twenty-five, John Dougan joined the Bank of Campbell.

The town, which you could only just call a town, one dusty main street with wooden buildings housing the local merchants, was growing, though.

Most of the inhabitants were connected one way or another with the orchards that abounded there and old man Campbell, after whom the town was obviously named, ran it with the help of the leading citizens, all of whom were God-fearing men. There were only two churches in the town, one for Methodists, the other Congregationalists. This was of no significance to John Dougan at first, because he continued to live in San Jose, and attended St. Joseph's.

He was content to start out as a teller, but it didn't take long for him to move up to be an assistant loan officer. He had a good understanding of the financial needs of the bank's land-owning customers and he developed a shrewd insight for a solid deal.

John Dougan was twenty-six when Cathy Hanson walked into the bank.

She recognized him straight away. He had filled out, of course, and his face had lost the young innocent look, which was to be expected. But he was the same John Dougan she knew from high school.

He was sitting at his mahogany desk discussing business - - she was sure it was business - - with Mrs. Jameson, a rather large, overdressed woman who, Cathy knew, owned nearly a hundred acres outside of town.

He leaned back in his leather swivel chair, smiled, and nodded his head at the woman as she explained whatever it was she was explaining. Cathy Hanson stood in line for the teller; she was in no hurry.

Dougan looked away from the woman and across the small, open office to the tellers' cages and he saw Cathy Hanson. He thought she was lovely, and although there was a familiarity about her, he couldn't place it. The noon sun was streaming into the bank through small windows and a shaft caught Cathy's golden hair and made it glow, or at least that's how it seemed to him.

She knew he was looking at her, and as she moved up in the line to the teller, she gave her best smile as she handed across her bank book and envelope of dollar bills.

"So you see, Mr. Dougan," Mrs. Jameson said, and John Dougan had to turn back to the business at hand.

He didn't actually see Cathy Hanson leave, but he sensed her lack of presence. It was a disappointment.

❦ ❦ ❦

The Bank of Campbell

Campbell Station was a very upright place, and Cathy Hanson had lived there all her life. Her mother, Daisy Hanson, had married Colonel Alexander McDonald two years after the death of her first hus-

Mrs. Daisy McDonald
The Colonel's wife and mother of Cathy Hanson.

band, John Harold Hanson. The Colonel was a man much revered in the community. A former journalist who had edited the leading dairy newpaper back in West Virginia, his presence at the local agricultural

The Colonel

shows was always an expected delight. His feelings for those less fortunate were well known and he became the first president of the Campbell Fruit Grower's Union Workers.

The Colonel had served with distinction in the Confederate Army under Stonewall Jackson, which no doubt gave him his commanding bearing and forthright manner. A leading member of the Campbell Odd Fellows, he was now retired and ruled the orchard ranch where the family lived together.

The estate was actually owned by Daisy McDonald, by virtue of her late husband's hard work and diligent responsibility for making a good will.

The Colonel had quickly become part of the elite group of elders who, with Mr. Campbell himself, organized the town and talked at meetings about its proper growth. The Southern Pacific railroad even stopped at Campbell Station now, with a direct line that ran to San Francisco and then with connections to Sacramento and the East. There was an exciting potential, provided everything was carefully planned and controlled.

The valley was lush with produce, labor was cheap. The climate was nearly perfect - - in short, it was a grand place to settle and raise a good family and business.

Nearby San Jose, on the other hand, was thought of as a very racy place. It had all the temptations no good person would want to be faced with, and it teemed with bars. The elders of Campbell Station did not hold with drinking, at least in public, and resisted the establishment of a saloon.

Which might have been one reason why Cathy Hanson's younger brother, Samuel, had left the town and gone south to San Luis Obispo.

The McDonald farm - - it was called Sycamore Ranch - - was at the end of town. There were neighbors living and farming off the rough dirt road that led up to the house. Beyond were the orchards and then into the rough country.

The house was a fine two-story building with a barn and outhouses. It stood on sixty acres, much of which was given over to cherry trees, apricots and prunes. The locals who had visited the McDonalds - - they were a hospitable and neighborly family - - thought the house was furnished in great style. There was an upright piano in the parlor and a large library well stocked with books.

While the property had been built by Mrs. McDonald's first husband, John Harold, the Colonel had done much himself to improve and add to its value.

Cathy Hanson loved the house and the orchard and while she had no particular ambition to take a career herself - - something the family might not have agreed to in any case - - she was genuinely interested in the running of the farm, the growing and tending of the fruit, its harvest and then shipment to market. In that way she took after her mother, although not in much else.

The Colonel and his wife approved of Cathy's involvement and so in a very comfortable way she began to learn the business side of operating an orchard estate, which, of course, was why she was now making calls at the Campbell Bank.

She would take the surrey when she visited the bank and in her summer cottons, demure but colorful, she looked the picture of the proper and very attractive California young lady.

"Good morning," Miss Hanson. "Very nice to see you again."

John Dougan was not exactly a conversational wizard, but in his dark banking suit and white shirt with its starched collar and bow tie, he gave an interesting impression. Cathy Hanson found him very handsome and felt she could sense in him some powerful undercurrent.

They passed the time of day together and John Dougan made the hesitant suggestion that if perhaps she needed any banking advice, why then, he would be very glad to offer all the help he could.

Cathy spent most of the time riding back to the farm trying to think up some not too transparent reason for asking John Dougan's advice.

❦ ❦ ❦

He was working on some loan documents when she came in. She went right up to the woman secretary and asked if she could make an appointment to see him. The secretary turned around and looked over at John Dougan. Then she asked Cathy Hanson to wait while she checked.

Well, she told her, Mr. Dougan could see her right away.

He stood up as she walked over and he offered her a chair. She looked wonderful, he thought. Their conversation revolved around the possibility of Cathy buying a small piece of land in her own name. Revolved was a apt description, because that is just what the conversation did - - it revolved around and around, using the right words; questions and answers, but as both of them knew, it was a manufactured facade created to enable them to sense each other out.

Her scent was pretty, her skin lightly tanned and flushed at the cheeks. His hands looked strong and capable. Her voice light, her manner shy. The way his eyebrows grew, and that magnificent moustache. She had a tiny birthmark on her neck, on the left side. The way he spoke, slowly giving thought to what he said. Her breasts under the feminine dress, not too small and a lovely shape. The way he leaned forward as if he might touch her hand. Her eyes, so blue and wide with wonder.

Messages to and fro and all the while a discussion they would never remember. It wasn't designed to be remembered; only the meeting.

"Well, Miss Hanson," he said.

"Yes, Mr Dougan?"

Did she ever do any wheeling, he asked her. She laughed and told him yes, when she was a child. On weekends he went wheeling - - he wondered, maybe? He could get her a lady's bicycle, he said. Just for an hour or so, and he could bring some food. No, she would do that, a few little things and a small picnic.

And so it started.

She read the society pages in the newspaper about the right things for a lady to wear when on a bicycle. He went to the Warwick Cyclery and rented a good machine for her, as light as he could find, and just for a moment he looked over a Rambler tandem they had there. It was $135.00 brand new.

He didn't take her too far; that wouldn't have been right. Mainly fairly close to town, where they could be seen. They talked endlessly, about their times at high school and how funny it was that they had never actually met there. He told her about his family and what had happened in Chico. They talked about the future, not yet a future together, but ambitions mixed with a little dreaming. All the stuff of young couples, finding out about each other. Trying to judge, and hoping each new attitude expressed would find sympathy.

The time soon came when she had to invite him home, for Sunday tea. It had been no secret, their meeting together; it couldn't have been in her family. On the face of it, the Colonel approved; he knew nothing about Dougan except that he was a local banker, an honorable profession. A man in that position could go far.

THE START OF IT

❦ ❦ ❦

Dougan, of course, cycled to the house. He wore his new suit for the occasion, the one he had bought from O. A. Hale & Company on South Second Street in San Jose. It was not an expensive one, it had only cost $10.00, but as he took good care of his clothes, saw that they were clean and well pressed, he looked smart. He left the bicycle up against the barn and he straightened out his clothes and combed his hair smooth.

She was waiting for him on the porch and they smiled at each other. She took his arm and walked him into the house to the front parlor. The Colonel was waiting for them, standing by the upright piano, his hands clasped behind the back of his Sunday frock coat.

Cathy introduced the two men and they shook hands. The Colonel, although a well-built man, was not as tall as John Dougan and he had to cast his eyes upwards when he spoke directly to him. Mrs. McDonald, who had been upstairs putting the finishing touches to her hair and watching out of the window for the arrival of Dougan, came into the room. She was an attractive woman, although a little overweight. Dougan could see the family likeness immediately. Cathy had her mother's fine cheek bones, he thought.

The introductory formalities over, Mrs. McDonald said she would bring the tea. The mahogany table was already set. The conversation was, as would be expected, very general, and centered around the season's crop, the weather and the prices of produce on the open market. All the while, Dougan was taking in the room, its tasteful and high quality furnishings, the warmth of the atmosphere. He would glance over at Cathy from time to time.

Mrs. McDonald carried in a tray and the two men stood up, the colonel taking the tray from her and setting it on the table. Cathy helped her mother pass out the cups and plates of cookies and home-made cakes. It was a scene that had been played out in the homes of young women for generations. A nervous young man calling for the first time. Trying not to make a mistake in his manners, trying to appear confident, but all the while awkward. The parents looking him over, the mother to establish that the young man was well kempt; clean hands, well polished shoes. The father asking business questions to assess his value: was the boy smart enough for his daughter, was he good enough for her?

Even if there was no indication that the friendship between daughter and the young man would amount to anything, the ritual had to be gone through - - sometimes frequently. Some young men became quite expert in the handling of the situation.

John Dougan commended Mrs. McDonald on her homemade cakes and she smiled and told him that Cathy had had a hand in the making. So it was established that her daughter knew about baking.

"They say you're quite a man for wheeling," the

Colonel said.

"Yes, sir," Dougan said. "Although I do ride a horse when the need arises."

"And you know the land?"

"Oh, yes, sir. Before entering the bank I worked the land."

"Ah, good experience. I hear you have a little property?"

"Yes, sir. A small farmhouse on the east side. I rent it out. The income pays for it, and as you know, sir, values are rising."

The Colonel smiled. "Very prudent, young man."

"Would you like some more tea, Mr. Dougan?" Mrs. McDonald said.

"No, thank you ma'am," Dougan said. Having got through handling the small cup and saucer and the delicate plates of food once, he didn't want to tempt the fates for a second time. He had had visions all the while he was cycling to the house of making a fool of himself by dropping a cup full of tea over what he imagined would be a very expensive floor rug.

There was a pause in the conversation and Cathy mentioned that Mr. Dougan was thinking of looking for a house in the area, so that he could be closer to the bank. The Colonel nodded; he was always pleased to hear that a man was the type to invest. It showed responsibility in a young person, to be thinking in that direction.

"I might be able to help you there," he said. He cleared his throat. "I have some influence, you know."

"Yes, I've heard, sir," Dougan said. "I understand you also have some stock in the bank." Dougan smiled. "In a way I suppose I'm working for you."

The Colonel waved his hand. "Oh, don't look at it that way, Mr Dougan. Just an investment, you know."

"Maybe I could show Mr. Dougan the orchard, father?" Cathy said.

"Yes, why not?" the Colonel said.

Dougan stood up and smiled at Mrs. McDonald. "That was a delicious tea, thank you, Mrs. McDonald."

"Oh, you're very welcome, Mr. Dougan," she said.

John Dougan turned to the Colonel and inclined his head, "Sir."

"Do come by the house before you leave, Mr. Dougan," he said.

The air outside seemed fresh and clear and Dougan let out a deep sigh. "Ah, well. That was interesting," he said.

Cathy laughed. "You were very good," she said, and she took his arm as they walked away from the house out toward the line of cherry trees.

Mrs. McDonald watched them through the parlor window. "They look a nice couple," she said.

"Yes," the Colonel said. "He seems a serious fellow."

In the company of Cathy, John Dougan soon forgot the ordeal of the ceremony in the parlor. Away from the house, in the open land, he felt secure. They walked and talked the afternoon away, and more and more Cathy felt the strangeness that an awakening was taking place. Dougan took off his jacket and carried it over his shoulder and the sight of his arms from under the short sleeved cotton shirt made her want to touch him.

Down at the end of an avenue of fruit trees there was a shed, a place where the workers kept their tools and their personal belongings while they worked the orchard. Sunday was the one day in the week when they did not work. John and Cathy walked towards the shed. She needed no prompting and moved with anticipation. When John tried the latch of the shed she looked back up to the house and then as the door swung open she moved to lean against the upright jamb.

"I love the smell of this place," she said.

It was musty with scents of the earth and animal fertilizer. Dust filled shafts of daylight came through cracks in the weathered wood planks and made patterns in the air.

His movements were tentative and uncertain, but urgent. His hand was on her shoulder, then in a flurry he was holding her and kissing her lips and face. They almost tripped over each other moving into the darkness of the shed.

"Leave the door open. Mind don't muss my dress."

There was no talk between them, sounds but no words. When he pressed her close with his arms around her, low so that one hand was on the roundness of her rump - - the feel of it was delicious and brought a rush of blood - - she felt his hard thing against her thigh. She wanted to touch it bare and squeeze it, then do other things to it. Things she had daydreams of doing to a man.

But she said "No," her voice low and hoarse. She felt him shudder and give a soft moan.

He was embarassed but the cold dampness on his leg was somehow a comfort and he felt strength too.

They gathered themselves, brushing imagined creases from their clothes, and then they walked slowly back to the house. The Colonel came out onto the porch and John Dougan tried to appear perfectly normal.

"Wonderful orchard and land, sir," he said, and he worried that his voice had taken a deep roughness that would betray him.

"Takes some keeping up, you know," the Colonel said.

"I want to thank you and Mrs. McDonald for your hospitality," he said.

"You're very welcome, young man."

John Dougan turned to Cathy and was formal in his thanks and she was the perfect young lady. There did pass between them though that look of secret relish only young lovers have.

He mounted his bicycle and waved to them as he rode off down the dirt road. In a way, he was glad to get away; conversation was not his strong point.

"Maybe we should invite Mr. Dougan to church next week," the Colonel said.

"I don't think so, father," Cathy said. "He attends St. Joseph's in San Jose."

The Colonel's expression changed, as did his

manner. "That's a Catholic church," he said.

Cathy laughed. "Yes, of course it is. John's a Catholic."

"I wasn't aware of that," the Colonel said.

❧ ❧ ❧

Colonel McDonald put into motion the influence he had told John Dougan he had in town. Enquiries, mostly, with people giving him bits and pieces of information. In a matter of a few days, he had almost a complete background picture on the man. As he told Mrs. McDonald, there was nothing specific you could put your finger on. Perhaps some kind of trouble up in Chico with a partner, but other than that, Dougan did not appear to have anything against him. He seemed to be quite a well-educated person, apparently he spoke German among other languages, although he did not go on to college after high school. That he came from a poor family was not the best of circumstances, but you could not hold that up to a man.

The man certainly seemed to be doing well for himself, and if it were not for the religious stigma, then there was little to which the Colonel could object.

What, if anything, did the colonel feel should be done, Mrs. McDonald asked her husband. The good man's conclusion was very little for the time being.

These flirtatious attachments have a way of dying out naturally, he told her. They would leave things alone, but keep a careful watch on developments.

❦ ❦ ❦

There were developments. Cathy contrived one way or another to see John Dougan, and he her. With each meeting they became more and more emotionally involved, and when John kissed her the feel of her skin on his mouth was like no other pleasure he could remember.

It was something close to a personal revelation for Cathy Hanson. Her whole upbringing had been the epitome of proper thinking and living. She had looked forward to courtship, an engagement, and after a suitable time, marriage and children. And in that order. A proper young woman saved herself for the right man. Those that didn't were considered whores, tainted by the devil's ways. Now here she was with the first man she really felt she loved - - just wanting him. It wasn't supposed to be that way; first came a mental compatibility, then gradually, and in the right time, there would be a physical consummation of that spiritual communion. What she felt was lust.

As she lay in bed those warm evenings thinking about John Dougan, her hands would creep under her nightgown to her breasts and she would caress them. With her eyes closed, she would dream it was his hands on her. Then she would put her hand down between her legs and massage the warm, wet place there until her body moved to its climax.

So when John Dougan suggested that instead of wheeling in the countryside that coming Saturday afternoon they cycle to his home in San Jose, she was eager to agree.

It was easy to arrange for George to be out for the afternoon, taking Jane, their sister, for a ride in the warm, fresh country air. It would do her good, John had said, and George, who had a pretty good idea of what was going on, went along with the idea. After all, John had done the same for him in the past.

The house in San Jose was simple and clean. It was a single-story, ranch-style wooden place with three small bedrooms, one for each of them who lived there. The furnishings were mainly common pieces, well polished, with lighting fixtures and ornaments bought from some market, but all of it in good taste. though. John Dougan showed Cathy into the parlor, which would also be the dining room if he and George ever entertained.

"Shall I make some tea or coffee?" he said.

"Not yet," she said.

She sat on the sofa, her arms stretched out along the back of it. He sat down beside her and her arms went around him, and they were kissing and his hand was slipping open her soft summer dress.

She helped him with the underwear she had bought specially for the occasion, and his mouth was on one

49

nipple, kissing it, while his hand caressed the other. Almost immediately, he reached under her long dress, pushing aside the folds of material until he was there. She felt for his thighs and undid the buttons of his trousers. Everything was urgent, two people almost grabbing at each other. She found him hard and squeezed him, and his body shook as he came with her touch. But he did not stop; with gasps of breath the pair of them stripped each other. Hands searching, helping, discovering.

There was no sophistication in any of it, in spite of their ages. It was a furor of exploration. All of it new to them. Unlike some first couples where the opportunity is taken tentatively, they seemed to relish a kind of mutual rape.

When they had to relax, their bodies damp with sweat, they sank down beside each other, exhausted from their exertions.

John Dougan felt stupid saying it and was embarrassed at the admission but nevertheless he wanted it out of the way, "I never did that before," he said. A man of his age, God, he thought.

She put her hand on his chest and softly moved it over his body, and she leaned over and kissed him on the mouth.

"Oh, I'm glad," she whispered.

Her hand went down his body and she touched him, fondled him in her hand. Already it was beginning to harden again.

"Oh, I just want to kiss it," she said.

While they were pulling on their clothes they

watched each other as if they could not take their eyes away. John was doing up the buttons of his shirt when he stopped, and reached over to take her by the shoulders.

"I love you, Cathy Hanson. Truly I love you."

He held her in his arms and tears were on his cheeks.

❦ ❦ ❦

After that first time they could hardly wait to be together again. They became almost reckless, and when Cathy came into the bank, it took all of John Dougan's restraint not to grab her in some personal place. On one occasion, Cathy even contrived to let her hand gently touch him, by chance it might seem, in his crotch.

She was surprised at herself, that she couldn't leave him alone, wanted him anytime anywhere. There had been a complete turnabout in her life, prim and proper girl one minute it seemed, then worldwide woman the next. And for John Dougan it was like he could suddenly see for the first time. Everything was a wonder. Neither of them gave it a thought that the first throes of love had engulfed them; they weren't up to thinking in any real way. Emotion had swept over them and taken reason with it.

If the Colonel noticed a change in his step-daughter, he kept it to himself. From time to time though, he did mention to Mrs. McDonald that he thought Cathy was spending a lot more time out of the house.

Long before the summer was at its height, Cathy told John Dougan she was pregnant. Suddenly the dreaming was over and the inevitability of hard reality intruded. Even so, in John Dougan there was a rush of excitement, almost of pride.

They were walking on the outskirts of town when Cathy told him, and the sun was warm and the trees in full foliage and John Dougan's face was happy and open.

"How do you feel my lovely girl?" he said and his arm was around her shoulder clasping her close to him as they walked side by side.

"I'm scared, John. I don't know how to think."

The tears were coming and Dougan held her and stroked her hair, and he looked to see who else might be there watching.

There was no one, but nevertheless he gently guided her toward the meadow on the other side of the dusty lane and they sat there in the shade of some silver birch.

"What are we going to do, John?"

He held her hand and squeezed it softly. "Are you sure?" he said.

"Yes, of course I'm sure."

"Oh, well I didn't mean to doubt . . . " He hadn't heard sharpness in her voice before. "You know, sometimes . . . I just wondered."

"Well, there's no more wondering about that," she

said. "It's a fact and something has to be done."

"Yes, I know."

"Well?"

He looked across the meadowland, a soft wind moved through the long grass and already the thought of a child was with him.

"John?"

He was almost startled by the sound of her. "Yes, there's some planning to be done," he said.

She was on her feet and there was a determination in the way she stood over him. "Planning? I've heard of some ways."

Now he too was standing, and the soft wind seemed to gather strength.

"I know what you mean and don't you ever say it again. Never. That is murder you are talking about."

"Murder of who, John? Who's there to murder? That can't be, not yet, it's too soon."

"How can we put a time to it?" he said. "When do we say what we created has become a person? In three weeks maybe or two months, or two months four days, five hours, six minutes and some seconds then suddenly, like God's constant miracle, a new person has arrived inside you that before was nothing."

They were moving, not walking, she touching the trunk of a tree then away from it, back again to lean, giving the tree her weight. John Dougan in the open grass, hands in the pockets of his pants, eyes down but when he had a point to make raised up and looking directly at her.

"Anyway, there's a law," he said. "You want to risk getting the Colonel involved, you don't want that now do you?"

He didn't want the argument, to talk about a soul, a human being. It was easier to keep to what was accepted, to what his church had decreed.

Cathy was facing the wind and it was strong enough to blow her hair back from her cheeks and to make the summer dress cling to the shape of her body. Her voice, although it was low, had determined strength to it and it was a side of her that John Dougan had not witnessed before.

"All those laws are men's laws," she said. "How can there be a law only for women made by men?"

She turned to Dougan.

"You carry and suckle the babies, then you make the law. And don't go telling me about that Pope in Rome, who's never known a woman let alone made a baby. What God gave him the right to tell me, a woman, whether to be mother or not a man's God?"

Her face was flushed and she faced to where the wind was coming as if the wind was speaking to her.

Then she seemed to be at the end of it and there came a calmness. "Oh, John, I'm sorry. I didn't mean to say all those things," she said, although to herself the words were well spoken - - and should be spoken, but for the fear of what they would create in men.

"I have to get back to the bank," he said.

They walked part of the way together.

"I'll have to tell them," Cathy said.

"I know," Dougan said. "You'll want me to be there?"

"No. I have to choose the right time and do it on my own."

Before they got to the main street with its store fronts and people, Dougan reached out and took her around the waist. "It shouldn't be like this," he said.

He smiled at her and his voice was uncertain. "I wanted it to be different, but would you, will you be my wife, Cathy?" The words came in a rush.

She smiled, and the tears began. "Yes, John. I'll be your wife."

❦ ❦ ❦

Mrs. McDonald didn't have to be told. She watched her daughter with a mother's eyes. It wasn't that she could actually read her daughter's face; it was the change in attitude, the gaiety and confidence that had appeared. When Cathy chose a time when the Colonel was out of the house to ask her mother to sit down and talk, then Mrs. McDonald knew for sure.

She did not cry for long. There was a toughness in that woman, a hardness, almost. She couldn't share her daughter's happiness or her anxiety. Her daughter was pregnant. A social disgrace. This person was to bring on her house and her family a terrible sin. How dare she. She did not hug her daughter to her, nor comfort her. Her first concern was what the Colonel would say and do. How could a daughter of hers do such a thing? The Colonel would kill that Catholic swine of a man.

Cathy was distraught. She had anticipated anger, that was understandable, but not coldness. The Colonel, of course, would be difficult, that was to be expected - - the upright head of the household, a man with a position in the community. Yes, that would certainly be a disgrace, but through it all she had thought she could count on her mother's support. Now, suddenly, she was on her own in that household. It was like her mother had closed her out.

"I will talk to the Colonel," the mother said.

The Colonel had had experience in matters that required cool, logical decisions. His journalistic background and the period he had served under the great Stonewall Jackson, these had prepared him for such times. He approached the problem like he would a campaign; he was a past master of the well designed strategy. He even went to the extent of drawing up written plans showing the options and the possible outcomes, and he sat for many hours, alone, in his book-lined study pouring over them; with the works of Shakespeare and other classics as company.

"What shall we do?" Mrs. McDonald asked him.

The only illumination in his study was from a single lamp on the mahogany desk. The lamp cast shadows in the room, across the richly furnished leather chairs to the floor-to-ceiling bookshelves.

The Colonel sipped his brandy. "I have made a plan, my dear. Mapped out a strategy."

His wife dried her eyes and smiled with attentiveness. She leaned forward in the chair and looked up at the Colonel who was now sifting through some papers on the desk.

"As we know, " he said. "The immediate problem is that Cathy is pregnant by a man totally unaccepable to either of us. I have been over the alternatives; killing him, having him run out of town, even a horsewhipping. But, my dear they are not wise actions to take. No, we must not make the mistake of direct opposition for that would lose you a daughter."

Mrs. McDonald relaxed, confident now that her husband had the matter in hand. He was skilled in the ways of understanding the minds of men, the army had taught him that.

"So, they must marry, and as soon as possible. But not in the Catholic Church. And that will be up to you, my dear - - to persuade her."

Mrs. McDonald nodded, pleased that she would be a part of the plan.

"Whatever happens there must never be a Catholic child of this union," the Colonel said. "My God, that would almost be worse than having a nigger. You must tell her that if she became a Catholic, and if anything, please God - - went wrong while she is with that child, the Catholic doctor is bound to save the child first - - even at the expense of the mother's life."

"Oh." Mrs. McDonald put her hand to her mouth in disbelief .

"Oh yes, my dear. The doctor would let the mother die to save the unborn child, that is their law."

The Colonel was pleased with himself, with his knowledge and the method of his approach to the problem. He took another sip of the brandy and then continued.

"Tell Cathy that if she marries into the Catholic faith the child will become the Church's, not hers. We must instill doubt into her mind. That is the way, for once doubt is implanted the way will be open for new thoughts and slowly we can work a labyrinth of suggestions and sow the seeds of erosion."

The Colonel smiled at his wife, "I will leave the details to you my dear. But, it must be done, and soon."

❦ ❦ ❦

The Colonel was a formidable man and he preferred circumstances to proceed with his guidance; he took great pains to guide his step-daughter and her mother. He was that way in all his dealings and had gained a reputation around town for being a shrewd man in a negotiation. His command of the subtle suggestion was a well practiced and insidious force.

There was hardly a time in the company of his step-daughter when he did not make some remark that related to her relationship with John and, more importantly, the Catholic Church. Like an endless rivulet of water that erodes the mightiest rock, he set about destroying whatever bond held the two lovers together.

So, the Cathy Hanson who went to meet John Dougan at St. Joseph's in San Jose was of a different mind than Dougan anticipated. In his simplicity he expected the same unequivocal surrender that had opened up in himself: to be bare and vulnerable to another person and to be without guile.

A man who thinks like that, of course, is due to be disillusioned, and the created disillusionment that had been brewing without his knowledge was about to make its irrevocable mark on events.

But, for that brief moment he was ecstatic. A wife - - he would soon have a wife. And perhaps a son. A boy he could teach. As soon as he was big enough he would buy him a bicycle and they would go wheeling together. He would show him his special trails and help him build his body so that he would grow big and strong.

In the meanwhile though, the arrangements had to be made.

The priest greeted the couple and his manner was friendly and generous. He showed them into his study, which was warm with mahogany and leather. They sat away from the priest's desk in deep armchairs that faced a fireplace piled high with unlighted logs. It would be a cool October before they would become a flickering fire. There was a low coffee table between, and John moved his chair so as to be closer to Cathy.

The priest, his name was Father O'Reilly, smiled at Cathy.

"Marriage, my child, is a sacrament, a sacred thing.

A holy bond for life. There is no divorce."

John Dougan looked at Cathy as the priest said that, but she never turned her head. Father O'Reilly moved on to the subject of children and their education. At that point Cathy spoke up.

"I must tell you, Father, that I am not a Catholic."

"I know, daughter. John told me. But you accept the written pledge of coming into the Church? And, God willing, should there be children, that they will be brought up and educated in the Catholic faith?"

She didn't reply, and stared into the unlighted fireplace.

"Cathy?" Her name came as a question from John Dougan.

"What would happen if I didn't agree?" she said.

The priest sighed. "Then I wouldn't be able to marry you in this church," he said.

There was an embarrassed silence. As far as John Dougan was concerned, the two of them had come there with the matter resolved. Certainly she had talked about it and told him her family was firmly set against the idea. But then she had agreed, gone along with him, until now.

"I can't do it," she said.

"But you said . . . "

"I can't, John, and that's it."

John Dougan didn't know what to say. He couldn't sit there and argue it out in front of the priest. He was stunned.

"Perhaps if you both took some more time. Talked it through," the priest said.

John Dougan stood up. "Yes," he said. "That's what we'll do."

They stood outside the church like strangers waiting on a street corner for a friend to come by and hoping they would come soon. Dougan took her arm.

"Let's walk," he said.

The afternoon sun was warm and lazy, and they walked slowly as if they had nowhere to go. Neither of them could talk. Now, suddenly they were discovering things about each other that before had been overshadowed by passion. Already, like a couple after the honeymoon, the business of living had intruded.

"I thought it was all decided," Dougan said.

"No," she said.

He felt hurt and betrayed. He was a man who, naively, believed the words people spoke. When, later, there was a contradiction, he could never understand it. He often felt that memory had little to do with truth.

"How could you wait until we were both in front of Father O'Reilly? Why didn't you tell me before?"

What made his religion so important, she wondered. God was God. Maybe the Colonel was right, the Catholics were different, an organized force to be reckoned with. It was funny, she hadn't really given it all that much thought until her mother and the Colonel had started telling her about them. Then, when the priest had actually asked her about the child - - her child, gotten down to the bare bones of it, to the hard reality of a decision, her upbringing decided for her.

"Oh, John, what's so important about getting married in a church anyway? Lots of people do it at home."

"It was important to me. You've been talking to your mother haven't you?"

"Of course I have. Every girl who's getting married talks to her mother, John. And particularly someone in my way."

It was the damn Colonel at the back of it, John Dougan thought. Getting at her and poisoning her mind against him. Giving her arguments all the anti-Catholics give.

"Is it because of that?" he said. "Because of the child?"

"That's part of it."

"All right," he said. "What is it you want to do?"

He knew that was not what he should be saying, giving in, he should be strong and manly - - in charge. But the thought of the child and his responsibility in its making once again made him see the other side of the argument. What to others might seem wishy-washy was to him fair-minded thinking - - seeing both sides.

She smiled at him. "Oh, John. We're going to be married, aren't we? What does it matter where?"

George Dougan was sitting on the porch having a beer when John got home. He could tell from his brother's face that something was not as it should be.

"Everything arranged?" George said.

"You might say so," John said and he went straight into the house. He was gone long enough to change and get a beer for himself, then he came back out and sat next to his brother.

"Well."

"She wouldn't agree about the child and right in front of Father O'Reilly," John said. "And after all our talking."

"What about the marriage?"

"Not in the church. In their home it's going to be, just her family and some of the hands. But you're still my best man, George. There's no question about that.

George was three years younger but in spite of this he was the more worldly of the two. He had had many women, went from one to the other, and he had never gotten himself into trouble. Well, not the kind of trouble John was in. John was a thinker and thinkers give themselves their own problems, George figured.

"I'll be your best man don't worry. You know who's reading the service?" George said.

"Their Protestant minister, I would imagine."

George finished his beer and got up from the wicker chair staring into the empty bottle. "I'm going for another, you want another, John?"

"Yes, I'll have another."

He knew what it would seem, that he was weak. May be, but the circumstances had to be known. Then another opinion would be formed, when the circumstances were known. It seemed he was thinking like that about everything now, acting in his way because of what he knew inside and not the way it would look to a person outside.

George came back with two bottles. He was drinking from one of them; he handed the other one to his brother.

"You rented that Campbell house?" he said.

"Yes," John said. "Signed the papers only yesterday."

"Well, you two get married and on your own, then when the baby comes along it'll change, you'll see."

"Yeah."

"Why don't you go back and talk it over with Father O'Reilly?"

John was resting on the banister of the porch, bottle of beer in his hand. "No use, George. I know what he'd say. It's a sin for me to marry outside the faith. As far as the Church is concerned, I won't be married at all."

"Have you thought of picking up and getting out of it?"

"Yeah, I thought about it. But, I don't think Cathy'd leave with me, and then there's the child who's coming." He swigged at the beer. "Going to be a father, George. Can't run out on that. And I want the child."

George was leaning back in the wicker chair that

was showing its wear from being out in the open air. Wisps of cane breaking off making sharp points that could hurt if they caught you the wrong way.

"You're right, you won't change her mind, not now - - not after that Colonel's had his say. Wouldn't want to go up against that bastard myself, I wouldn't."

"Maybe I'll have to," John Dougan said.

George thought about it. "John, there could be danger in all of this. I mean real danger."

"Yes, I know."

George swigged at the bottle some more. "I want you to know, John, that whatever happens you can count on me. Even if it looks as if maybe you can't - - understand?"

"Yes," John said. "I understand."

❧ ❧ ❧

The parlor of the McDonald ranch house was adorned with white sweet pea blossoms and smilax. On either side of the fireplace were jardinieres filled with white lillies. Ferns and potted plants were grouped in the nooks and crannies of the room.

Cathy Hanson wore a rich dress of cream white - - not pure white - - corded silk trimmed with Mechlin lace. A spray of white blossoms was arranged in her hair and she carried a bouquet of Niphetos roses and ferns. She was beautiful.

She came into the room on the arm of the Colonel,

who was dressed in his formal black frock coat. The wedding march was being played on the piano by Cathy's younger brother, Samuel, who had come up from San Luis Obispo for the occasion.

There was no bridesmaid or maid of honor. Mrs. McDonald stood on the left side of the minister. She wore a white and blue striped silk dress trimmed with lace. Her only ornaments, other than her own wedding ring, were a string of perfectly matched pearls around her neck and a diamond ring on the third finger of her right hand.

John and George Dougan stood waiting.

The service was simple and short and it was taken by the Methodist minister. There was no sign of joy or tears as would be expected, just resignation. Even the two ranch hands standing by the side of Mrs. McDonald were untouched by the service.

Mrs. McDonald served her usual homemade tea and she and the Colonel chatted with the minister. For the rest, there was an awkwardness. Cathy introduced her brother to John and George and they made small talk about the goings on in San Luis Obispo. Samuel treated the brothers with in-difference.

It was not what anyone would call an auspicious start to a marriage. After the formalities were over the newlyweds rode in the surrey to the rented house that John Dougan had taken on the outskirts of town. As the Colonel had pointed out, they had already had their honeymoon.

The small wooden house was partially furnished,

enough to start out with and John Dougan, who was making arrangements to buy the place eventually, would take Cathy into San Jose where they would shop for curtains and sets of crockery and all the things that newly married couples buy together to make their home. It had already been agreed that Cathy would have the child at the ranch house, where her mother could be with her, and the Colonel had said that he would take steps to hire a nurse, at his expense, to look after Cathy and her child.

The McDonalds never called at the Dougans' house; excuses were always made but John Dougan knew it was a deliberate slight - - one of many to come.

To all intents and purposes they lived as any normal, young married couple who were expecting a baby. Except that most days, when John was at the bank, Cathy would ride over to the ranch and spend much of the time with her mother and brother, Samuel, who had decided, now that Cathy had moved out, to stay and work the ranch with the Colonel. There were even occasions when John Dougan would come home to an empty house. Once a week they would be invited to the ranch for dinner. They were not good times for John Dougan.

With Samuel home there was quite a group sitting around the table, passing plates of vegetables, gravy for meat and other accoutrements of the meal. The conversation would be the usual talk about the orchard and so on and it would be led by the Colonel. John Dougan was not part of that and if he interjected

John Dougan with His New Bride Cathy

some piece of news of his own, while it might not be received with total silence, the response was never enthusiastic.

It became a terrible feeling that he was always the listener. The way Mrs. McDonald arranged the place settings at the table, Samuel was on Dougan's right with the Colonel, at the head of the table, on his left. It was as if Dougan were the interloper between the two men, the words crossing from one to the other.

"The harvest looks like it's goin' to be a good one," Samuel said.

"Yes," the Colonel said. "Now don't you prefer being back home, Samuel?"

Samuel smiled across the table at Cathy. "Sure. Gotta be near my big sister."

In an effort to be included in the conversation, John Dougan spoke up. "Business is picking up at the bank."

He was ignored and, as if to reinforce his lack of inclusion in the family, Mrs. McDonald immediately turned to her daughter.

"Cathy dear, remind me to show you the knitting I've been doing."

"All right, Mama," Cathy said.

John Dougan knew it would be a waste of time to make another attempt to join in. So, he just sat there within himself.

"Seems we're to have a new doctor in town," the colonel said. "Coming west with his family. They say he's a good man. No doubt he'll be joining us at the Oddfellows."

Samuel turned to John Dougan and with his mouth still full with food he said, "Your people don't hold with you joining the Oddfellows now, do they?"

"No," John Dougan said.

Samuel leaned over the table, reaching for his wine glass, and his hand seemed to fumble for the glass and then it was over and the red wine was spilling on the table cloth. The wine splashed and some of it went onto John Dougan's coat and trousers.

"Damnit," Samuel said. "Gettin' clumsy." He did little to conceal the smirk on his face, and there was no apology.

John Dougan said nothing, and he took his napkin and started to dab at the wine stains.

"Oh, John, go use some water," Cathy said. "You're just rubbing it in like that."

He pushed his chair back from the table, mumbled his excuses and then left clutching his napkin. Dear God, he thought, he could smash that brother, really smash him. But he said nothing, just left the room.

The Colonel watched John Dougan leave and then he turned back to the table and with his voice low, "They say this doctor wants to tell us about a society called the American Protective Association. Says it was formed to stop the Catholic take-over. There's been some terrible things going on back East, Samuel," he said. "There's going to be a meeting, you should come."

Samuel nodded in immediate agreement. "I'll be there Colonel, don't you worry," he said. "Just tell me the time and place."

Cathy's Brother Samuel

The Colonel looked up as John Dougan came back into the room. Then he made a play of wiping his mouth and beard with his napkin. Just look at him, he thought, what a sight his clothes, all damp patches.

There was nothing John Dougan could do to hide his self-consciousness. He sat back at the table and pushed the plate of cold food away.

"You all through, John?" Cathy said.

"Yes," John Dougan said. "I'm all through."

❦ ❦ ❦

He started making a practice of stoppng in at the Belloli saloon after work for a beer or two to prepare himself for the evening ahead. There was also the chance that he might meet and talk with friends who would listen.

"I'll never understand," he said.

"Yeah, they're a mystery all right," the other man said.

The man was about the same age as John Dougan, although he looked older. Rougher, too, probably a farmer with his cowboy boots and work clothes.

"You've been married?" Dougan asked him.

"A couple times."

"Well?"

"They was both very similar I would say, in a manner of speaking; after the bloom had worn off and they figured they had me all sized up and trained to their ways of thinking."

"Seems they change, like become a different person."

"Oh yeah, you're right there, they change an' with

memories only as good as the last little present you bought'em. But they never forget it if they don't get it their way. Not until they got their own back."

He lifted the glass and drank the beer. "They always get their own back, you can count on that. See, I reckon we's the weaker sex if you ask me. Women, they're tough."

"They can get so cold," Dougan said.

"That's their way," the other man said. "Strong weapon indifference, wreck a man if he'd let it."

Dougan turned to the bar and lifted his arm. The barman saw him, and Dougan showed two fingers. "You gonna have another aren't you?" he said to the other man at the table.

"Oh sure, I'll take another."

The barman brought the drinks and the two men sat hunched over them and silent, both thinking about their own worlds and talking to the other was really talking to themselves.

"I'm a Catholic," John Dougan said, "And that's the trouble."

"Oh."

"She isn't, and her family they hate Catholics."

"You seem all right to me," the man said, "but then I'm not much of anything myself."

"It was good at the start."

"Always is," the man said, "they turned her did they?"

"Yeah."

"Families'll do that, in-laws'll kill yuh."

"She's got a step-father, he's the one behind it."

"I had one of those once, nearly killed him myself."

"I'd never go that far," John Dougan said.

"You don't know how far you'd go if there was provocation enough."

"No. I got to get her away, after the boy comes."

"What boy?"

"My son, she's pregnant. I gotta have my son brought up in the faith."

"How the hell you know it's goin' to be a son?"

"I just know, always have right from the time she told me."

The man laughed and beer spilled onto his chin.

"Shotgun was it?" he said.

Dougan was laughing.

"Yes, that's right, would have been that for sure, except I didn't need persuading."

The man hardly knew Dougan, seen him around town occasionally and at the bank when he went there. But they had cottoned to each other over a couple of drinks. There had been times, in the past, when he had needed someone himself, a sounding board as much as anything, who would put up with the depression he had and even though they would be bored would give up their time, and sometimes their solace. So, he figured it was his turn to pay that back.

There was something pathetic about Dougan, he thought. Came over strong that he really loved that woman and she was turning him away and he was feeling deep hurt. All over some damn religion, he'd seen it before and never understood it really. He'd keep an eye out for him if he could.

"Guess I should be going," Dougan said.

The man looked up, "See yuh again?"

"Yes, I'll be by, always about this time."

"Don't you go doin' anythin' foolish now."

Dougan smiled, "No, I won't."

❦ ❦ ❦

The envelope was marked personal. It had been left on his desk by the secretary. The handwriting on the single sheet of notepaper inside it was strongly formed and easy to read.

Dougan, the note started out. Be good enough to meet me outside the Oddfellows Hall tonight at eight.

That was all. It was signed by the Colonel.

The meeting was on his mind all that day. Was this some kind of reconciliation, an offer maybe? Or an ultimatum?

It was a cool night and Dougan wore a jacket. He did not take the road but the brush and wooded land that skirted it. He moved well and silently like an Indian stalking; he was at home there. Outside the Oddfellows Hall the Colonel waited by the surrey. He had arrived early, he was a punctual man by nature. Every sound in the still night alerted him, although he was disciplined and did not show it.

Dougan could see the outline of the building, then the surrey. He had heard the horses before then. He watched. The Colonel had come alone.

The Colonel didn't see Dougan until his dark outline took its shape as he stepped out from the trees.

"Good evening, Colonel," Dougan said.

The Colonel stood as if he expected to be saluted.

"Good evening," he said.

"Well, I came," Dougan said.

"So I see."

The Colonel began pacing, his two hands clasped behind his back. A set pattern, up and down, making a trodden path and scuffing at the leaves. Dougan stood his ground, his eyes never leaving the moving figure, like watching every move of a predator.

"This has got to come to an end," the Colonel said. "I'm prepared to be generous."

Dougan had nothing to say.

"Damn it, answer me."

"Would you demand a colored turn white, or a Jew become a Christian?" Dougan spoke slowly and deliberately. Actually he had rehearsed the words in an imaginary conversation days before. He had been doing a lot of that, making up conversations in his mind, and he was determined, if he could exert the will power, to keep to the mental scripts he created.

"She wouldn't have been seduced by a dark skin or Semitic features, by what she could see." There was a hate and disgust in the Colonel's voice, it was as if even just the thought of a black man or a Jew being close to the white skinned girl was enough to bring up his bile. "Your kind keeps what they are hidden until they choose to speak of it or cross themselves."

Dougan hadn't put those words into the Colonel's mouth in his make believe confrontation. For a moment he wondered if he detected a hint of possession. Could that be, with her married and pregnant? Then he could feel the anger rising in himself at his own thoughts.

"There's goin' to be no end to this," Dougan said. He was anxious to have it over. "No point in talking about it, you made up your mind right from the start anyway. Nothin's goin' to change that."

"Why don't you go away, get out of all our lives?"

"You want I should leave my child who's coming? You want me to give up what any half decent man wants?"

"Half decent? You give yourself graces. No Catholic is even part decent. You defile the air you breathe. You do what I want, Dougan, or your regret will be sudden and no less than you deserve."

More than the words it was the very proper way they were delivered that made John Dougan shiver. The cold, blatant fury of the man. He knew that given the circumstance the Colonel would see him dead, do it himself if need be.

He had never before faced a man with such open festers nor looked into the eyes of a person and seen such hate burning there, and all because of a belief.

The Colonel turned and climbed into the surrey. "I came to be reasonable," he said. "To make you an offer, but I can see it would do no good."

He looked down at Dougan and he grasped the reins tightly, and the horses strained them; anxious to be moving. "But I tell you, Dougan, there will be no Catholic in my family whatever has to be done."

❦ ❦ ❦

Then the American Protective Association came to Campbell.

The A.P.A. did not arrive with a band and waving banners. The new doctor moved in and opened a practice. He was a man from Michigan with a wife and family who had come West. Because he was a professional person, he was taken up by the local elders and it was not long before he started talking about the way the Catholics were beginning to make a mark for themselves in California business and politics.

It seemed to him and the others that a new group of people, people not of their kind, were gaining some success. This disturbed them and was another fear to add to the growing list.

Fear of the black man and what he might do, fear of the Jew, fear of the Irish, the Italian, the Spanish. It depended on what you were as to what you feared and hated.

The doctor showed them the A.P.A. publications and then he arranged for an ex-nun, he said, to come and talk to them about the evils of the Catholic church. The printed and the spoken word fell on fertile soil and the movement began to flourish.

It was not long before it was almost a requirement to be a member. If you were not, you were either Catholic or sympathetic to their cause.

It was good business and good politics to be with the A.P.A.

The McDonald family virtually became charter founders. Even Cathy went to one of the weekly meetings. John Dougan, back from his college studies, would find an empty house yet again.

As the weeks went by, he became a silent, brooding man. The torture of being ignored became an unbelievable burden. He knew most men would have packed up and left, they wouldn't have taken it. But there was a stubbornness in him; he wanted to see his child born - - wanted it to be brought up his way.

It became an obsession. He would beat them all out in the end.

❦ ❦ ❦

The barber shop on South First Street near San Antonio was empty except for W. K. Johnson, who sat in one of the barber chairs reading the morning *San Jose News.* John Dougan pushed open the door. "Good Morning, Bill," he said. "Right time for a trim?"

Bill Johnson wrapped the white cotton cover around Dougan's neck, then he lowered the chair. Dougan was a man who sat upright and tall in a chair.

They went through the usual formalities of asking

about each other's family, and they commented on the weather and the state of the local economy. And then Dougan brought the conversation around to Johnson's studies. Johnson would not be a barber for much longer, because in all his spare time he was studying to become a lawyer.

The young man was enthusiastic, and while he combed and cut Dougan's hair, he talked on about completing his studies and about the excellence of the teaching he was getting from an attorney, John Goss, who also happened to be Dougan's lawyer.

Dougan listened carefully and the two men would glance at each other in the mirror facing them.

"Mr. Goss says he's working well on that fore-closure of yours on the Penn property you own," Johnson said.

"That's good," Dougan said. "It's a sizable amount, fifteen hundred dollars, and I could find a good use for it."

Dougan seemed to turn the conversation away from himself, as if what was happening to him was of no consequence. He asked the young barber more and more about the law, and what he had learned; what kind of practice he would go into when he passed the Supreme Court examination in August.

It seemed just by chance that they got around to talking about inheritances and family wills. The young lawyer-to-be was flattered to be asked, particularly by a banker, and he would frown and give a question apparent deep thought before he answered.

He stood back from Dougan's head, comb and scissors in hand, and delivered his opinion to the mirror.

"There's no doubt about that Mr. Dougan," he said. "It's the rule of consanguinity. If a man's child is the sole survivor of an entire family, then he or she would inherit the whole estate." He felt proud about his store of knowledge of the law, and his scissors cut swiftly and cleanly.

Dougan then began to talk about the studies at Santa Clara he was embarking upon, of how he was to push himself to complete Greek and Latin language courses in half the time it would usually take. Then after that, he would himself perhaps turn to law courses, and maybe he, too, would become a lawyer.

"That would be a fine combination," he said, "banker-lawyer."

The barber-cum-lawyer had finished with Dougan's hair and leaned over him to trim the thick moustache, and to curl its ends.

"There, just about done, Mr. Dougan," he said. "Really, you didn't need too much of a cut."

John Dougan studied the back view, and then handed the mirror to Bill Johnson who took it and lifted the cotton cover from him with a flourish, and then brushed the loose hairs from Dougan's collar.

"Yes, ... I know," Dougan said. "But I like to look tidy."

81

The Warwick Cyclery was not far from the barber's. Dougan wheeled his bicycle into the shop, and left it propped up against the counter. The cyclery was as much a meeting place - - almost a social club for the local enthusiasts - - as it was a business. The manager, Shelly, was standing around with some customers and friends discussing a newspaper article.

"John," he said. "Have you seen this?" And he held up the open pages of the paper.

"What's that?" Dougan said.

Shelly laughed. "Well, it's something that would appeal to you sure enough."

The other men there laughed too, because they all knew that John Dougan was the most serious wheeler in their group. It was said that he had once cycled from San Diego to Campbell.

"Why don't I read it out loud?" Shelly said.

He looked over at Dougan. "This writer has a fine plan, John," he said. He started to read from the paper.

"'I am working,' the article states, 'upon the greatest bicycle scheme that ever agitated the sporting fraternity. Little by little we conceive great ideas and develop around them. Each sounds more preposterous than the last, but when we bring it all around, all who came to scoff remain to admire. This wheeling scheme is the finest thing ever thought out by a wheeling man. It came up at one of our meetings by chance. And I have looked into it and found it feasible.'"

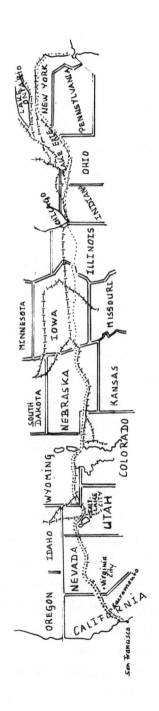

The Trans-Continental Bicycle Tour from Ocean to Ocean on a Wheel

This Trans-Continental Bicycle Tour goes through twelve states, touches the principal lakes and rivers and can be accomplished in forty to eighty days.

Shelly looked around the place as if to check that everyone was listening. "Go on with it," one man said.

"'The scheme, the writer continues,' Shelly said, 'is this: to establish a bicycle track from coast to coast so that wheelmen can journey from San Francisco to New York as easily if not as rapidly as they now do by train. Such tours have been undertaken and partly carried out. My plan of a route runs like this: I would start, say, at the Pacific Coast, and going north from San Francisco, would strike across for Sacramento. Once in Nevada, I would keep pretty close to the railroads to steer clear of the Santa Rosa Mountains. The railroads have mapped out things pretty well along there, and I should hug the track, taking only excursions by the hour all through Nevada and Utah until I reached the Great Salt Lake.'"

Shelly put the paper down. "Well, what do you think of that, gentlemen?"

There were mumbles of approval. "And here the writer has a map." Shelly spread the paper out over the counter and the men crowded around to view the map that outlined the routes. It was captioned, "This Trans-Continental Bicycle Tour goes through twelve states, touches the principal lakes and rivers, and can be accomplished in forty to eighty days."

"How about it, John?" Shelly said.

John Dougan looked up from studying the map. "I think, as the writer says, it's perfectly feasible. If you had the need to do it," he said.

Dougan moved away from the group over to the rack of new, heavy-duty tires. Shelly left the men reading the rest of the article and he and Dougan got down to the serious business of selecting a set of tires, heavy-duty wheels and spokes. They talked to each other with authority and at the end of it, Dougan walked out with two new wheels, the extra strong spokes to go with them and a pair of thick, extra strong tires. He would assemble them all himself, he said.

When he had left the store, Shelly turned back to the others and said, "Looks like John Dougan is set to take a rough trip. He sure is an organizing man, that man."

❧ ❧ ❧

Cathy Dougan was at the sink washing out clothes when John got home to the rented house. Her pregnancy was showing with the full roundness in front and her gait, as she walked, was getting to be a slow roll.

"Hi there, darlin'," Dougan called out and he was struggling with a big package coming through the door and being careful with it. He put the package on the kitchen table and went and kissed her on the cheek and all the while his hand was on her rear.

"John, just leave me alone when I'm working. You're always touching me, fiddling around."

"That's 'cause I love you darlin'."

85

"Well all right, but all you seem to think about is touching."

He knew there was no point to keep doing it so he went back to the package and sat at the table and started to unwrap it. He was careful and when the wrapping was off he lifted what was the picture of a bicycle and held it at arm's length. "See now, what do you think of that?"

She looked back over her shoulder and her hands still in the sink with soap suds up her arms. "It's a bicycle," she said and her voice was flat without any enthusiasm.

"Sure it is," Dougan said. "Honey, that is a Rambler tandem. Brand new, that's a $135 bicycle. I was thinking of getting us one."

"Yeah, well who you going to have ride on the back seat?"

"Why, you, darlin'."

"Not now you aren't," she said and she went back to her washing.

Dougan sat and studied the painting and while it was more like a poster than a piece of art he got satisfaction from it. The bright colors the artist had used, shining just like they would be on a real new bicycle. Deep reds and browns and the metal work without a mark on it.

"That's a real life-like rendition that is," he said. "I'm going to get our son a bicycle soon as he's old enough. Teach him all my wheeling ways."

"And what makes you so sure it's going to be a son?"

"I'm sure of that," Dougan said.

"Mother came and visited today."

Dougan nodded his head.

"I'm going to the house to stay until the baby comes."

She was wiping her hands dry and she sat at the kitchen table, her feet splayed out and flat on the floor. She leaned back in the wooden chair, her hands with the towel folded around them cradled in her lap.

"The Colonel's hired that nurse for me."

"You said he would."

"It's the best thing, John - - doin' it this way."

"Yeah, I suppose it is. "

For a moment she felt for him; felt his isolation. The moment passed.

🍒 🍒 🍒

It was dark when George rode up to the house on his bicycle. He leaned it up against the porch and then he called out.

"You in there without any lights on, John?"

He heard shuffling, then the porch door creaked open. "Yeah, that's right, George. Nothin' wrong about the dark when you're on your own."

He waited and listened as John went back inside and then the lights were coming on all over the front of the house. He went up the steps now that he could see them and he saw straight away the bottles in the

87

bathtub of ice on the floor next to the dining table.

"Plannin' on a party?" he said.

John was not doing too good on his feet.

"Help yourself, George," he said. "There's plenty to be had."

The two sat at the table drinking straight from the bottles and anyone passing by would see them through the front windows of the house and if they wanted to stay watching they could count empty bottles.

"She's up at her mother's permanent now?" George said.

"That's right," John said. "The Colonel hired a nurse for her, to take care of the baby when it comes, and the mother she moved downstairs and gave over the upstairs room so the nurse can be in it and right next door to Cathy. They got it all organized they have."

"I heard some talk in town about this American Protective Association you told me about."

"Yeah, remember I told you they got a kind of fear we're going to take over or something."

George laughed out loud and he banged the beer bottle on the table. "Take over what, for Christ-sakes?"

John leaned across the table and his head jerked forward like it does when a person who is nodding off catches themselves doing it. "I got me a plan," he said. He made the words dramatic, although they came out sounding slurred.

"Yeah," George said. "I got one for you too. Become a Jew."

John hooted with laughter and then they were both laughing to where they couldn't stop it seemed and tears were coming down their cheeks and the more they tried to stop the worse it got.

"Become a Jew," John said between the laughs. "That'd be worse than what I am now."

"The only thing worse than what you are now would be being Colored."

They were both clutching at their stomachs and John nearly fell off the chair, and George was choking on his beer. Then when they realized the noise they were making they began to quiet down some.

"Oh, my God," John said. "Oh, God, you ever met a Colored Jew, George? Now that's a thing you don't get many of I reckon."

George was too exhausted to laugh and he sat shaking his head and his upper body was still quivering.

"Bet one of those would make a hell of a market man. He'd sell more pumpkins at farmer's market than any white man ever would."

"How many white Jews you know are farmers?" John said.

"Now farming's not a profession the Jews take up you know that," George said. "They don't wanna get their hands dirty so you could see the dirt for a change."

They went on drinking until they had no energy left for talking or making fun and it never occurred to them that what they had said to each other was what they hated to hear.

❦ ❦ ❦

The sun was warm on John Dougan's back as he sat on his haunches and spun the wheel of the bicycle, tightening or loosening the spokes to make it true. While his concentration didn't waver his mind was on snatches of made-up conversation and arguments that flitted in and out of his mind until he would stop and shake his head as if that would stop the bombardment of twisted images and voices.

What to do and how? The early days of a child. They were the most important, when your ideas became their ideas. You shape them in those early years, give them something of yourself.

They didn't want that, they wanted their teachings to influence the child. Dougan spun the wheel and the spokes were a blur. A man might not accomplish much in his life except be a father to a son or daughter. If someone wants to take that away they might as well take away the man himself and be done with it.

At first he thought the sound of the horse was another figment of his imagination, but it was real and suddenly there were swirling clouds of dust and the clatter of sliding hooves on the hard, stone-strewn ground. Dougan squinted his eyes and looked up through the murky sunlight. Samuel was above him sitting on the sweating horse like a conqueror come to finish off the enemy.

"They sent me over," he said, his breath coming with difficulty so that the words came out rough.

"What for?"

Samuel wheeled the horse and it reared its forelegs startling Dougan so that he lost his balance and fell back onto the ground and the bicycle fell too. The brother shouted back over his shoulder at John Dougan. "She's started early. Doctor's up at the house. You can come up if you want."

Dougan looked after the horse and its rider as they raced down the path and through the trees on the way back to the house. Then it was quiet and the dust was settling. Dougan got himself back on his feet and he pulled up the bicycle and sat it firm again resting on the upturned seat and the underpart of the handlebars.

He had been insulted again, but there was no time to dwell on that and he brushed the dirt from his clothes, then rushed into the house for his jacket. He would leave the bicycle, it would take too long to reassemble it, and he would run there. That's what he would do, run.

The doctor's surrey was waiting outside and Dougan was up the steps and into the house without waiting. He was collecting himself and brushing down his clothes when the Colonel came into the parlour. He looked serious.

"There's nothing you can do," he said. "The doctor and the nurse are with her."

"I want to know how she is," Dougan said.

"Right now she's doing fine. You'll just have to wait. Like the rest of us."

The Colonel turned and left the room and Dougan knew he was right, there was nothing he could do but wait. He slumped into the high-backed chair, closed his eyes and tried to calm his raging mind.

The child was born at four o'clock in the morning.

Mrs. McDonald herself had been sitting on a wooden chair in the upstairs corridor, opposite the room in which Cathy, the doctor and the nurse were watching and waiting on the child's arrival. She heard the slap and the first sounds of a baby crying, then Nurse Hisler opened the door to look out into the dimness.

"Are they both all right?" Mrs. McDonald was on her feet.

"They're just fine," Nurse Hisler said.

"Thank the Lord. A boy or girl?"

"A lovely boy," the nurse said.

Perhaps there was a fleeting shadow that crossed Mrs. McDonald's face.

The sound of voices brought the Colonel and Samuel up the stairs and the three of them followed the nurse into the room. They were told to hush their noise by Nurse Hisler.

Cathy was lying in the bed gently cuddling her new baby. The doctor was putting his coat on and he looked up at the group come to see the child. He smiled, "Mother and child are doing well," he said.

Mrs. McDonald moved close to the bed and she smiled at her daughter and grandson. "Oh, my, he's a lovely looking sight."

"Husky fellow, considering he decided to arrive early," the doctor said.

"Anyone mind if I see my son?" John Dougan was

standing in the doorway in shirt sleeves and his hair was tousled from sleep. He didn't wait for a reply and started to cross the room. He had to wait for Samuel to move out of his way so that he could get to the bedside.

He looked down at his wife and son and his voice was husky.

"God bless you both. You all right, Cath?"

There was the hint of a smile on her face.

While he was standing there, intent on the sight of his wife and son, Samuel left the room and the Colonel turned to the doctor and told him he would see him out. The doctor asked the nurse to follow them and then Mrs. McDonald joined the group in the corridor outside the room.

John Dougan really saw his son for the first time as the dawn sun flooded into the valley from the east and lighted the room. The wrinkled face was clean and shining and his head had a fine covering of dark, down-like hair.

"Good looking son we got us there, darlin'."

Cathy smiled at him and then looked at the boy and tightened her arm around him.

"Don't touch the child." The nurse had come back into the room.

John Dougan did not look up at the nurse. "That child is my son," he said, and his voice was deep and uneven and his breathing quick and shallow as he tried to hold back the emotion that had filled him. He could not hold back the tears that came to his eyes.

"Mrs. McDonald would like to see you, Mr.

Dougan," nurse Hisler said. "I think your wife should have some rest."

"Yeah, I guess she does need to rest," he said and he leaned across the bed and kissed Cathy on the cheek and then he gently touched his son's head with his lips. "The Lord be with you, my son," he whispered.

Mrs. McDonald was waiting in the corridor for him.

"I think it would be wise if you held off visiting for a while," she said.

"You telling me I can't come and see my son, Mrs. McDonald?"

She breathed deeply as if to control herself and the words she said were spoken slow and deliberately. "My daughter's been through a lot and had a rough time of it - - in more ways than one. She's going to need all the peace and quiet she can get."

"I won't be disturbing her, Mrs. McDonald. Not me."

The child was baptised in the Methodist church in Campbell Station.

The Colonel could now barely tolerate John Dougan. He was too much of a gentleman to allow his feelings to show in company, but deeply woven into the family fabric were the threads of a persistant distrust and growing hatred. As he stood there in the church watching the proceedings, and hardly being able to diguise his disgust at the sight of John Dougan standing by his step-daughter and the minister, he had at least the satisfaction of knowing the child would not grow up a Catholic.

Cathy Dougan, nee Hanson, who was now up and about, but still living at the ranch, held her four-week-old baby in the crook of her arm with tenderness and smiled down at the boy. He was being good. Already she could see a likeness to John, his father. She had tried to keep her thoughts of the future out of her mind. But when she looked at her son the memories came back. Why, oh, why did it have to be like this?

When the minister asked who would name the child, John Dougan's voice spoke out clear and firm, and as he gave the names, he felt the warmth of his love for the boy.

❦ ❦ ❦

Living apart had changed them, he thought. She was out of his sphere of influence, and the small things that people do together, that closeness brings, had no chance to nurture or develop. As there was no natural being together; when he visited her at the ranch it was like two friends meeting. They could tell each other their news, and they would talk about the boy. He felt like he was visiting someone in the hospital where you sit by the bedside initially enthused with your first flush of news which, when exhausted, wanes and falls into silences which you try, unsuccessfully, to avoid.

Every time he asked when she and the baby were coming home, she would be evasive.

"It's been nearly two months, all told," he said. "And I miss you Cathy." His voice sounded plaintive to her.

"And I miss you, too, John, but just a little longer. It's scary, having a baby, you know that? Picking him up when he cries and not knowing what to do right."

In the end, he felt she would never come back. It was her family, he was certain. They had her and they had the baby - - they had stolen everything from him.

The Colonel was pleased; so far everything had gone the way he planned. Mrs. McDonald had been superb, she had gained Cathy's confidence completely - - come to terms with her over that Catholic's bastard son and convinced her, he was certain, that for the child's sake, he would be better off with the family. Which, of course, he would - - that boy would be very rich some day.

As for Cathy, she wondered at herself how one could change. Having the baby had probably done it; things were different when you suddenly had your own child, as if the man who had given it to you was no longer necessary. And her mother had been good.

She changed, too, and again was warm and loving to her.

She felt secure at the ranch and the thought of going back to John's place - - not their place - - made her scared. Not physically, for herself, but for the baby. The Colonel had read to her papers that told terrible stories of what lengths the Catholics would go to keep their children in the Church.

John wasn't the same as before, either. He had grown sullen and strange. He would avoid anyone in the family, would hardly talk to them if he could help it. What to do about it, though, troubled her. But her mother told her not to worry, the Colonel would take care of everything, she said. She had no need to worry, none at all.

❧ ❧ ❧

John Dougan parked his bicycle outside the Belloli Saloon on the corner of Third and San Fernando Streets. He went into the saloon and walked through to the back of it, and sat at a table in the dim shadows. The waiter, who knew his regular drink - - a dark beer - - brought it to the table. When Dougan went to pay for it the waiter nodded to a man across the room who had lifted his glass.

Dougan smiled, he recognized the man from before. He took his drink and went to join him.

"Thanks for the beer," he said.

97

"My turn, I remember," the man said. "Heard you had that son you were expecting."

"Yes, we did," Dougan said. "And a fine one he is too."

They drank together. "Ah well, it's a good day," the man said.

"Maybe not too good," Dougan said. "Take a look at this." He handed the man a printed pamphlet.

The pamphlet was on A.P.A headed paper, and it outlined a state of panic that had taken place in Toledo, Ohio, where, it said, the A.P.A. had been forced to buy a consignment of guns to protect the inhabitants against the possibility of a Catholic uprising.

The man raised his eyes, looked hard at Dougan, sniffed and then went back to the pamphlet.

During the night and day, for seven days, the pamphlet ran, the Ohio soldiers, fully uniformed and armed, stood in readiness at the Toledo armory for any outbreak that might occur. Portions of three companies of militia, one company of cadets, and one of artillery, which constituted the city's military force, joined in. Detachments from all units remained at the armory guarding the ammunition and Gatling guns.

The man threw the pamphlet back onto the table. "Exaggerated horseshit I would say."

"Maybe it is," Dougan said. "But there's plenty of copies circulating around town. And to top that, I hear 'em saying the A.P.A.'s coming out for the Republicans."

"McKinley'll get the nomination without them," the man said. "Don't you worry."

"They're even coming out against him," Dougan said. "Saying he put many a Catholic into office. Two million members, that's what they're claiming. Two million, that's a lot of people."

"Blown up bigger than it is," the man said. "They all do it. Wouldn't think there were more than a few thousand in the whole country if you really knew the truth."

"It doesn't matter what the truth is," Dougan said. "It's what people believe."

They talked on about the power of the A.P.A. to arouse hatred against Catholics. The man was inclined not to take the matter too seriously, but Dougan was totally obsessed by the idea of the secret society, which was no longer so secret, and what it could accomplish. He started then to talk about his own family, and what it was like to be in the middle of a group of Protestants who not only were church-going members but staunch supporters of the A.P.A.

"They're shutting me out," Dougan said. "They'd do it to the boy if he were old enough, and they're getting to Cathy real good. Making her believe I'm some kind of devil. Even the ranch hands are going to meetings with them. I don't know how much more of it I can take."

"The A.P.A. trouble'll pass," the man said. "These things always do. You wait and see what happens in the East. First the membership'll drop off and then a few politicians who used the movement for their own gain'll give up on them too. Then they'll all fade away."

"But what happens to me in the meantime?" Dougan said. "It doesn't matter what happens in the East, goddamit, it's what matters in my own place."

"What are you going to do?"

"I got some plans," Dougan said.

The two men sat over their drinks, each lost in his own thoughts. Dougan's mind a turmoil, the man more concerned about his crops than for any threat from some supposed secret society.

But he worried about Dougan. He was a changed man, that was for sure. Could have seen some of it coming ahead of time, though. Catholic man marrying into a Protestant family, that was ready-made trouble. Religion had ruined many a marriage; ironic really he thought, as all religions were supposed to be based on love.

"John," he said. "You'll see, this will all die down, everything changes sooner or later. Why, believe me, there could even be a Catholic president leading this fine country one day."

Dougan drank the remains of his beer, put the glass back on the table, and lifted his large head. "Never, there will never be a Catholic president of these United States. They would never let that happen, they would kill him, someone would."

Cathy Dougan sat on the seat of the swing that hung suspended from a thick and weathered branch of the oak tree out back of the house. It was warm, even in the late afternoon shade of the tree. She kicked at the ground with a toe and the swing moved gently back and forth. While she held onto the ropes she didn't really need to steady herself. She was enjoying the sensuous movement of the swing, her thighs open and the forward motion making her think of John. Then she heard nurse Hisler coming from the house and she smiled in anticipation.

"Here he is, Miss Cathy. All nice and sweet."

She laughed then and went up onto the veranda and took the child from the nurse's arms. "You're so good with him, Mary."

"Always been that way with babies. Now men they's another thing."

The two young women laughed and Cathy thought that for a poor white girl Mary had some of the colored's gift for fun. Maybe there was a streak of tar in her family somewhere.

They both turned as a surrey came into the yard and a young woman with long brown hair, slim and tall with a pretty face that was tanned from the sun, stepped down.

Cathy laughed and handed the child back to Mary Hisler.

"Here Mary. Take him for me." Then she was back down the steps and she and her visitor were hugging each other.

"Jessy," Cathy said. "Jess-y, you look just

wonderful."

"And you too, Cathy, mother and all, and I want to see him, Cathy. Let me see your baby."

They were giggling like the schoolgirl friends they used to be.

Nurse Hisler held the child and Cathy reached over and gently pulled back the shawl. "There," she said.

"Oh, he is so cute, isn't he just?" Jessy said.

"You want to hold him, Ma'am?" Nurse Hisler asked and she felt as if she were showing off a prize of some kind and she wondered why the mother wasn't doing the showing off.

"Oh, no," Jessy said. "I'd be afraid I'd drop him."

At that John Dougan junior started to cry.

"Maybe I'd better take him in. Time for his sleep anyways," Nurse Hisler said.

Mary Hisler carried the child back inside the house, and she sat on a chair and cuddled and rocked him in her arms and he stopped crying right away and outside his mother was laughing with her old school friend.

"Now tell me all your news," Jessy said.

"What news? I had a baby."

"Was it bad?"

"It wasn't easy."

"What about John?"

"Lets walk a bit," Cathy said.

They walked towards the orchard where the hands were still working. Although they didn't go close enough so that they would have to pass the time of day.

"It's no good anymore, Jessy. He's changed, like a different man, and the Colonel - - well, you know. The Catholics, the whole thing - - it's terrible, frightening. I'm frightened of him, Jessy. He wants the boy. That's all he talks about - - his son. Not me, I don't count anymore. Just his boy and wanting him brought up Catholic."

"Well, he's your husband, Cathy."

"Oh, I know, Jessy. But, I can't go back to him - - back to that house we were in."

They came around to the end of the path that ran alongside the small orchard, before the big acreage of fruit trees started, and Cathy turned and started to walk back toward the house.

"Oh, well the Colonel's going to take care of the whole thing; he and Mama."

She smiled at her friend and held out her hand to be squeezed.

"Never mind, Cathy. It'll turn out all right in the end," Jessy said.

"Look at the fruit," Cathy said. "Aren't they lovely. We're going to have a fine harvest this year, that's for sure."

❦ ❦ ❦

Colonel McDonald arrived at the bank before it opened for the day's business.

The guard unlocked the door for him. "Good morning, Colonel," he said.

"Good Morning, Bowden, I'm expected," he said. He stood upright and rigid, his gaze never leaving the manager's door ahead of him. Not even a glance to acknowledge John Dougan's presence.

The manager came from his office to personally welcome the major shareholder to the site of his investment.

"Good morning, Colonel. How good to see you again."

The Colonel followed the manager directly into his office and the door was closed behind them, after the manager had cautioned his secretary that they were not to be bothered under any circumstances.

John Dougan saw it all, of course. Sitting at his desk, he could see out onto the entire banking floor. Not much could go on there that he did not notice.

The tellers, who were preparing their stations, started whispering to each other, "That's Colonel McDonald, owns most of the stock, " the older one of them said.

The other glanced back at John Dougan. "Didn't he marry the daughter?"

"Step-daughter."

"I hear they're not living together, and a new baby."

"Not right from the start, that marriage."

He had known the Colonel was coming, had an appointment with the manager. A point had been made of it to all the employees. His imagination was at work and all the fears that could come into his mind came. Oh, to be able to listen to what was going on behind the closed door.

To everyone's surprise the meeting was a short one. They had imagined that the Colonel would be going over the bank's business or perhaps discussing some expansion plans - - the bank was doing very well: deposits were up, trade was brisk, and so some planning would be afoot. John Dougan knew better.

The two men came from the office, they shook hands and the Colonel left; as simple as that. It was kind of an affront, there being a reflected glory in having a very important person on the premises. If they do not stay long you can feel let down, that some fault is yours.

Immediately after the Colonel left, the manager called John Dougan into his office. There was flurry of excitement among the staff.

The manager, who was a very proper man, came straight to the point.

"You understand, Mr. Dougan, that what I am about to say is as the result of orders. We all have to take orders, directions from our superiors."

John Dougan nodded. He had an idea of what was to come.

"I am afraid, ahhm . . . I am sorry to tell you, Mr. Dougan, that the bank is dispensing with your services."

John Dougan stood up. "When do you want me to leave?"

"At the close of business today. I've been instructed to draw up a generous settlement."

So, this was it, Dougan thought. This is what it

had come down to, first they take his wife away, then his son, now his job - his position in life. What does a man have if all that goes? He has a shell that's all, an empty shell.

"You understand, Mr. Dougan?"

The bank manager's voice brought him back to the moment.

"Yes, thank you," Dougan said. "I'll need all I can get. Now I've got me a son to take care of."

Part 2.

THE MURDERS

THE LEGEND OF JOHN DOUGAN

John Dougan left his bicycle in a clump of trees across from the Odd Fellows meeting lodge. Even in the darkness he could recognize the wagon and some of the horses that were tethered outside the wooden building. He was careful about the way he walked over to the building; for such a well-built man he moved easily - - like a hunter.

He stopped for a moment and studied the rough-drawn notice nailed to the entrance of the meeting hall.

His long, lean body was poised to move swiftly.

The slightest movement or sound, a cat stalking some mouse or a bird rustling in the trees, produced a sudden turn of his head, nervous eyes that flashed and a tightening of muscles. Then, once he knew there was nothing to fear, his body would relax again.

He moved closer to the building, up to one of the small, open windows in the side of it. There was no drape pulled over it and he peered into the lighted room, careful to hold his face back from the glass so that no one inside could notice him standing there.

He knew most of them; many had come to the bank. He studied the faces but when his eyes, moving over the rows of people, came to the front they hardened at the sight of his in-laws. The very upright Colonel and his wife, and next to them, her son, Samuel. He didn't recognize the speaker who was standing in front of the assembly. Probably some traveling representative from the East, he thought. Kansas City most likely.

He could hear the speaker pretty clearly. In his hand were copies of A.P.A. newspapers, *The Patriotic American* and *The American Citizen*. The speaker would wave them at his audience as if to make a point.

"Now," the speaker said. "I am going to read out to you good people an oath. An oath you should learn by heart, and I'll give you copies of it to take with you when you leave, because when we next meet I will expect those of you who wish to join this secret society to make that oath with all your soul's yearning."

The fear the speaker's words evoked, even though he had not actually said anything fearful yet, swept over John Dougan. He had to make an effort to control his body from shaking.

"Listen carefully," the speaker said. Dougan watched as the Colonel nodded to his wife and her son, to ensure that they paid good attention to what was to come.

"I do most solemnly promise and swear," the speaker said, his voice low and earnest so that his audience had to lean forward in their seats, eager to catch every word.

"That I will always, to the utmost of my ability, labor, plead, and wage a continuous warfare against ignorance and fanaticism; that I will use my utmost power to strike the shackles and chains of blind obedience to the Roman Catholic Church from the hampered and bound conscience of a priest-ridden and church-oppressed people; that I will never allow anyone a member of the Roman Catholic Church to become a member of this order, I knowing him to be such, that I will use my influence to promote the interest of all Protestants everywhere in the world that I may be; that I will not employ a Roman Catholic in any capacity if I can procure the services of a Protestant."

The Colonel was nodding his head and frowning, and his lips were tight beneath the thick moustache and beard that covered more than half his face.

" . . . I furthermore promise and swear that I will not countenance the nomination, in any caucus or convention, of a Roman Catholic for any office in the gift of the American people, and that I will not vote for, or counsel others to vote for, any Roman Catholic, but will vote for only a Protestant, so far as may lie in my power . . ."

John Dougan could take no more of it, and he staggered back to the clump of trees. He stood there in the dark and shivered. He must leave before the meeting was over. He struggled to mount his bicycle and then he rode out into the dark night.

❧ ❧ ❧

The moon was full and the sky clear, so that the cold white of the moon lighted the open land and cast deep, black shadows into the tree-filled orchards that lined the dirt roadway. It was only a little over a mile to the McDonald ranch on the outskirts of town. Dougan took his time. The air was warm and there was no wind; it was a pleasant night to ride. Inside of him there was a rage burning.

The ranch house and the barn were like black slabs in the colorless night. There seemed to be nobody about. He could hear the horses in the stable and the surrey was over by the stable too, so he knew Mrs. McDonald had come back from the meeting. She would have had to come on her own; the men stayed late, discussing ways and means of what to do with his Catholic kind. They would walk back from the

A.P.A. meeting at the Odd Fellows Hall on a night like this.

He went quietly up onto the porch. The door was open, and he walked into the house. The white ice of moonlight made sharp shadows across the floor of the hallway. He could see into the parlor. There was no one in there. They would be in bed by now. Mrs. McDonald in the downstairs bedroom at the far end of the corridor, the nurse and Cathy and his boy upstairs.

He could hear the grandfather clock ticking, and it struck the half-hour. The sound came clean and pure in that still night.

He started up the stairs, going carefully so as not to make too much noise, but that house was built solid and there were thick carpets everywhere, and attached to the walls were pistols and antique muskets, and even further up, Indian weapons and axes. They were all part of the decoration in that fine house. Cathy's bedroom door was open a crack, probably so the nurse could hear her call out in the night or hear the baby if he woke.

He pushed the door open and in the moonlight he could see his boy fast asleep in the crib and Cathy asleep too in the bed beside it. He walked over to the crib and bent down over it. He smiled. There he was, fast asleep, his boy. Cathy mumbled in her sleep and turned and John Dougan went to the foot of her bed and stood there watching her.

Even asleep, she was beautiful, he thought, tousled up under the covers. He really loved her; they had some good times and there would be more, too, when he had his way.

Cathy moved again in bed, as if disturbed, and then with a sudden twist of her body, she sat bolt upright. Ahh! She put her hand over her mouth to stiffle the sound. Then she relaxed as she recognized the tall dark figure at the end of the bed.

"What are you doing?" Her voice was a nervous whisper.

"I came to talk," he said, and he kept his voice low.

"In the middle of the night? My God, you scared me half to death."

"We have to go, Cathy," he said.

"Go? What do you mean, go?"

"Now. Get away. Be on our own again with the boy."

"You must be mad. Now, at this time."

"No. It's right. You're mine and he's mine."

She felt a flight of fear shudder through her, him standing there, half in the moonlight, half in the dark, tall and strong. The men wouldn't be back yet, she thought, or he wouldn't be there. "Go home, John," she said. "Go home, and we'll talk about it tomorrow."

"No." His voice was raised.

"Be quiet, you'll wake the baby."

He came around by the side of the bed and he sat on it, close to her.

"Cathy, what's happened?" He stretched out his hand to touch her face and she moved back from him.

"John." There was a tremor in her voice.

"I just want us to be happy together, away from here," he said.

"Where would we go?" she said. "You want me to pack up right now?"

"We'll just leave," he said, and there was a boyish enthusiasm in his voice. "Go back to our house. We can borrow the surrey."

"Where are we going? I said, where do you think we're going?"

"Home, Cathy. You, me and the boy. We'll go home."

"This is home," she said, and looked down at the cot. "And this is his home, too."

"No, Cathy."

"Yes, John. Yes it is. You've ruined everything with that damn religion of yours. I won't have it. I've asked you, how many times have I asked you? Oh, but you won't change. No, not John Dougan."

He couldn't understand her. They had loved each other, and even now he wanted her, but she went on talking against him, kept on and on, wouldn't let him alone, wouldn't even listen to him. On and on she was going, her voice still low, but keeping at him, telling him what a fool he was, ruining everything. As she ranted at him, it seemed to him that her face had changed; the beauty went out of it and now there was ugliness. She wouldn't stop talking, on and on. And when he tried to say something, she would look away, ignore him. That was the worst of it, being deliberately ignored. Trying to talk to someone who looks away to the corner of the room, and not at you.

He just sat there on the edge of the bed and she wouldn't listen to him, kept looking away, wouldn't listen to him, wouldn't even look at his face. And he kept talking and she kept looking away, and he was talking to nothing. Nothing, he was talking to nothing; nobody.

"Listen woman." No, she wouldn't listen, she didn't want to listen.

"I'm talking to you, woman, I am talking to you, woman, woman, listen to me, I am talking . . ."

He reached out to touch her again, to hold her so that her face would look at his face, and she twisted away and he held her, ". . . talk to me!"

She twisted and he held her and then he stood up and he was still holding her. And then there was a crack like a dry twig had snapped.

Suddenly it was all so very quiet.

She was still. There on the bed, very still. Her body not looking right somehow, her neck not right. Then the door was open and the nurse Hisler was there, screaming, and she was screaming, and he pushed her out into the corridor to be away from his boy, and she was screaming and as his hand went up the wall, to steady himself, and he clutched a handle and he pulled it and he hit the nurse, and he kept hitting her, and there was blood everywhere. The blood was on the floor and on the wall and on him, and he kept hitting her until she was quiet too, and on the floor in a pool of blood.

He heard the cries coming up from below. Nervous cries, nearly screaming. It was the mother - - she must have woken up. She was at the foot of the stairs as he came down, and she saw the bloody axe in his hand and the first thing that went through her mind was that he must of taken it off the wall. She recognized it; they'd had it for years and she had put it on the wall herself, along with the other antique guns and things.

Then he was suddenly on her and she was screaming and put up her hands and arms to protect her head, but she couldn't stop the blade of the axe and John Dougan crashed it into her skull. There was a cracking as the blade went into her skull and then the blood was spouting out and the axe hit her again and again and again. Her head seemed to swivel on her neck and her false teeth came loose and as she fell the teeth slipped out of her mouth. She looked like a grotesque old doll on the floor, a doll covered with its own blood and its hair smeared and caked over its open skull. The broken teeth were on the floor beside her and her shriveled face was the color of tallow and red paint.

John Dougan rushed back up the stairs to Cathy's room, past the body of the nurse. He went over to the cot and stood over it. The boy was asleep. He looked down at his son and he clutched the axe handle and he lifted the axe and seemed to study the blade that was covered with the blood of the two women.

"You'll be free soon, my son," he whispered to the child.

It was very quiet in that house and he heard the grandfather clock in the hall chime the quarter-hour. It had seemed like no time at all to him. Everything so fast, without thinking. What to do now? What to do? The men, yes the men, they would be back, but maybe not for an hour or so. Mustn't stand around though - - things to do.

He didn't even look down at the nurse, just stepped around her and the blood-smeared floor - - careful not to tread in the blood. He went back down the stairs again and he stood looking at the body of the mother. He had better move it or the men would notice it as they came through the front door. So he leaned the axe up against the grandfather clock and he started to drag the body down the corridor to the bedroom. She was easy to drag and he was strong. He didn't take care with the body, dragged it like a sack of potatoes, right into the bedroom. Then he came back into the hall and got the teeth. It went through his mind that maybe he should stick them back in her mouth, but he didn't bother. Just placed them besides her.

As he looked up he saw himself in the bedroom mirror. His face was all bloody, so were his clothes, and his hands were bloody too. He went to the sink and he poured out some water from the pitcher there, and he washed his hands and face. There was nothing he could do about his clothes. Well, the blood was nearly dry anyway.

He seemed completely unaffected by what he had done. Perhaps that was because he wasn't finished. She had started it, really; she shouldn't have treated him like that, and he her husband. Anyway, once under way, it had to be completed, couldn't leave yet. No, things unfinished. All be a waste now if he didn't do the job properly.

He went through Cathy's belongings looking for photographs of them together and photographs of himself she had somewhere. He found them in a chest of drawers and he took them. Then he went to the Colonel's study to search for the pistols he knew the man kept there. He found them in the drawer of the desk together with a box of extra shells. The guns were already loaded and he pushed them into the waistband of his trousers.

Well, he could wait now. He was all prepared. Just wait for them to get back from their meeting. All that talking they were doing about Catholics, talking into the night. Now there would really be something for them to fear, and talk about. They would open the special bottle of Southern Bourbon and would pour out a nightcap. They would be getting more than a nightcap, more than they bargained for, those two.

He sat in the Colonel's chair, the axe cradled in his lap. He would let his hand caress the polished wood handle of the axe. He would hear them coming in that still night.

It was nearly twelve midnight as the Colonel and Samuel walked up the dirt road to the ranch. It had been a good meeting; Mrs. McDonald would have enjoyed the plans they had made, might even have contributed to them. Samuel would be glad to get home; he could use a drop of the Colonel's bourbon. The two ranch hands who had gone to the meeting with them stayed in town having their nightcap at the Belloli Saloon.

He could hear them. Footsteps on the porch and then the door was opened. He got up from the chair and went and stood behind the parlor door, up against the wall. The light from the moon seemed to flood the room, a pale light without any warmth. He was a tall, dark shadow against the wall.

Samuel came in first and Dougan let him go on into the room. Then, as the Colonel followed him in, Dougan brought the axe down on his head. The axe blade hit the Colonel high on the side of his face, just above the eye, and as it struck him, he let out a scream. The blow sent him crashing into the piano and as he put out his arm to save the fall, it hit the keys, and as he slid to the floor, his hand brushed over them, making discordant scales.

The stepson turned at the Colonel's scream and lunged at Dougan. The axe came down again, but Samuel managed to grasp at Dougan's wrist and deflect the blow. The two men grabbed and thrashed at each other, chairs went over, ornaments smashed, and as they crashed into the wall, pictures fell to the floor and were crushed. Dougan tried to hit Samuel with the axe and twice he missed, ripping into the plaster wall.

The Colonel could do nothing. There was blood pouring down the side of his face and he wiped it away so that he could see.

The two fighting men fell suddenly, and the axe flew from Dougan's hand. Then Samuel was punching at Dougan's face. He was sitting on his chest, punching and punching away. But he was not as strong as Dougan and the big man threw him off. As Samuel staggered away, Dougan looked up from the floor at his black-silhouetted figure and he drew his pistols. He kept firing them, and in the dark night some of the shots went wild but he hit Samuel, hit him five times, three times with the .38 and twice with the .45 revolver. The last was at close range, so close that the powder from the gun scorched Samuel's coat and it was over for him.

The Colonel had managed to get to the door before Dougan had finished and he clawed his way down the corridor to the kitchen. The window was open and he crashed into furniture in his desperation to get to it before Dougan could catch up with him. He was leaving a trail of blood and he smeared it on the window sill as he climbed through and out into the open air.

He started shouting for help. The ranch hands should be back by now. The Colonel ran across the open ground to the ranch hands' cabin, shouting all the way. Dougan came out of the front of the house and he could see the colonel clearly. He was less than two hundred feet away when Dougan started firing.

As the Colonel made the door of the cabin, Klaus, the young German hand, ran across to the barn. He got inside before Dougan saw him and he climbed to the loft above. He stood shivering at the door in the loft as he peered down to watch the scene below. Dougan was at the door of the cabin and he fired into it, the bullets splintered the wood, and the young German heard the Colonel cry out for help.

Dougan stood outside the door, both guns in his hands. His face was covered with the marks Samuel had given him and there was blood all over him.

He shouted at the door. "Come out, Colonel, come out. I've got to have you."

"Don't shoot anymore, John. Put them up and I'll come out."

"All right, Colonel. I'll do that," Dougan said.

As the Colonel staggered out into the moonlight Dougan shot him. The Colonel's body twisted as he made an attempt to turn back to the cabin, and Dougan shot him again, and again.

The Colonel was dead. Dougan could see that as he stood over him reloading the guns. He turned and went to the cabin door and kicked it open, and from the other side of the partition that divided the room he heard the crash of glass as the other ranch hand, Joseph, dived through the back window. Dougan shot him through the broken glass, twice in the back.

There's another one, Dougan thought. There's one more.

"Klaus, where are you?"

The young German crouched back from the loft door. He was petrified.

Dougan walked over to the barn and went into it. Klaus could hear him below, searching. He heard the horses and there was a rustling and he thought he could hear Dougan slowly climbing the ladder to the loft. He couldn't stop himself from shivering. There was nowhere to hide. Maybe he could rush him as he got to the top of the ladder, push him back off it.

Klaus
The hired hand who escaped John Dougan's intent.

That was the only thing he could do, if he had courage.

The ladder moved.

Then he heard one of the horses being led out of the barn - - it must have knocked the ladder as it went by. The young German crawled to the loft door and very slowly and carefully he looked out. Dougan was directly below him. He had harnessed the little buckskin mare, but there was no saddle on her. He watched Dougan mount the horse. Dougan seemed to wait, looking around. Then he was off and away.

The young German leaned back against the loft door and vomited.

❦ ❦ ❦

Leonard was in his bedroom reading when he heard the commotion. His window was half open that warm night, and at first he thought it was coming from the windmill that needed greasing. But when he went to the window he heard the screaming, "Murder, help, he's killing me!" He recognized the Colonel's voice crying out and he heard John Dougan's reply.

He didn't take time to dress properly, just pulled a pair of overalls on over his bare body, then rushed downstairs to get his next door neighbor, Gregory Page. Together they roused another neighbor, Albert Whipple, and the three of them banded together and went over to the McDonalds' ranch.

The firing had stopped and it was quiet. They didn't see the body of the colonel because they went straight up to the house. The minute they opened the door, they could smell burning. It was coming from the parlor, and Leonard struck a light and they went into the parlor.

Wisps of smoke were coming from the body on the floor.

"Good Jesus Christ," Whipple said. The room was a shambles. There were broken pieces of furniture, glass from pictures, and crockery and blood everywhere. One of them got a pitcher of water and poured it over the body of Samuel McDonald. He was an ugly, frightening sight.

"One of the shots was at close range," Page said. "Set his clothes smoldering."

"Someone should go for the Sheriff," Whipple said.

"I'll go," Page said. He was glad to get out of the place.

The other two men decided to search the upstairs part of the house and when they got there, the shock of what they saw made them reel back in horror. The pool of blood was still soggy around the head of the nurse, Hisler. They were strong men, men who had worked on the land all their lives, and they were used to a hard life, but this was something the likes of which they had never seen before.

In that quiet night there was a sudden whimper. It came from the cot.

"Good God, it's the child," Ross said.

They went to the cot and Whipple bent over and raised the boy, held him in his arms. "Thank the Lord," he said. "The baby is all right."

Ross could hardly hold back the tears. "His dear mother, Christ, his dear mother is dead."

All Whipple could do was hold the baby and look down at its tiny face and shake his head from side to side. It was unbelievable, neither of them could comprehend what had happened there.

"I'd better take care of him," Whipple said, his voice low and hoarse. "Someone has to take care of the poor mite. I'll take him to my wife."

They left the house in a daze, not knowing that if they had gone back downstairs to the back bedroom, they would find another body with its life beaten out of it. As they were walking across the open ground the young German, Klaus, came out of the dark.

"It was Dougan," he said. "Dougan killed the Colonel, killed Joseph. Oh my God, he killed them all." The young man was staggering like he was drunk and the words kept tripping out of his mouth. "Terrible, oh God. I couldn't do anything. He would have got me. In the loft. He came to get me. Like a nightmare."

"All right, boy," Ross said. "Where did he go?"

"He rode off, he rode off. On the mare, just rode off minutes ago."

"Come to the house," Whipple said. "You need a drink, boy."

He looked at Ross. "We all do."

Sheriff Lyndon came with a posse of armed men.

They rode onto the ranch and hitched their horses and they spread out to search the place.

"Leave everything," Lyndon said. "Leave everything for the coroner."

It didn't take long for them to discover the bodies, and they found the .38 on the porch where Dougan must have thrown it before he rode off. It was a sight none of them had ever witnessed before. They had seen killings, shootings, knife fights and the like, but nothing, nothing close to what had happened there that night.

It was like some animal had ravaged the place and the people. There were blood stains everywhere, across the floors, on the stairs, the piano, the window sills, everywhere.

"We have to get after him," Lyndon said, and just then a young man pushed his way through the crowd of men. "Sheriff Lyndon," he said. "I talked with Dougan only half an hour ago."

"What did you say, boy?"

"I did, I talked with him."

"Just quiet down, men," Lyndon said. "I want to hear what this boy has to say." He turned back to the young man. "Go on with it."

"Well, I was out walking. Coming up here after I'd heard, you know, about the killings."

"What's your name? the Sheriff said.

"Joe Reed, sir."

"All right, Joe."

"As I said, I was walking - - down by Campbell Avenue and the Los Gatos Road - - and this man came riding up and he seemed in a state."

"What kind of state?" the Sheriff said.

"Like he'd been in a fight. His face was all bloodied and cut and he was riding bareback. I asked him if he'd heard about the trouble at the McDonalds' place, and he said who's McDonald? I thought that was strange 'cause everyone around here knows the McDonalds."

The Sheriff waited. "What then?"

"He just rode off down the Los Gatos Road, and that was it. But I recognized him. He was John Dougan all right."

The young man paused for the dramatic effect. He was enjoying his moment of glory. "There's one more thing, Sheriff," he said.

"What?"

"He didn't have no boots on. His feet were wrapped in rags. I noticed that right off."

The Sheriff was an organized man and he set about sending parties of men out to scour the nearby countryside, and he got out telegraph messages and he notified the railroad company. By that time the grounds of the ranch were filling with people come to gawk. They were coming from all over the county.

"Constable Thomas," the Sheriff said, "I want this ranch closed off. Keep everybody out except our people and the coroner when he arrives."

"The newspaper reporters from the *News* are here, Sheriff," the constable said.

The Sheriff allowed them in and he gave the grisly story, or what was known of it. "He can't get far," he told the reporters. "We'll have him by morning."

But they did not have him by morning, nor by evening.

❦ ❦ ❦

George Dougan rode up to the McDonald ranch and tethered his horse off the road by the path leading into the orchard. He pushed his way through the crowd gathered around the entrance to the ranch. Constable Thomas was stationed at the gate and he stopped George Dougan from going through.

"I'm George Dougan. I had to come," he said. "I couldn't believe what they were saying, what he had done."

A murmur went through the crowd when they heard the name.

"He did it, all right," the constable said. "There were witnesses."

"He must have gone insane," George said. "He'd never do such a terrible thing in his right mind."

"Insane or not, he did it," the constable said. "And we're going to get him for it. There's already reports he's been seen. And I'll tell you another thing, there are people in town talking up a lynch party for when he's brought back."

There were grumbles coming from the crowd and some of them pressed forward and started to jostle George Dougan.

"Let him be," the constable said, and he raised his

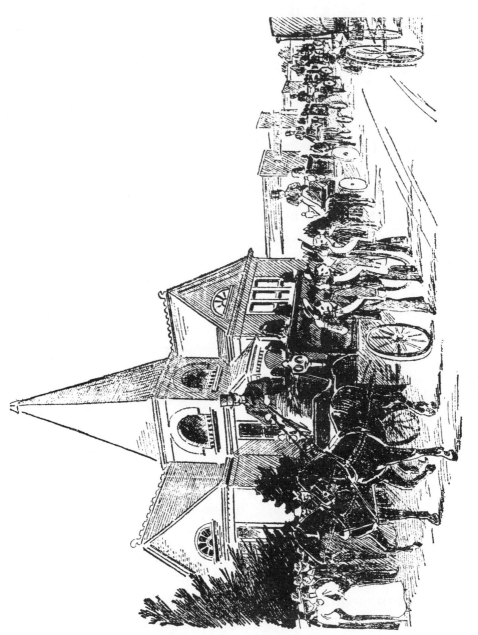

Five Hearses in Line

rifle up across his chest, his finger over the trigger guard.

"Horrible," George said, and he looked back into the crowd. "I want him caught as much as you."

"You had better leave," the constable said. "Let him through there," he called out.

The crowd opened a path between them and George Dougan walked back to his horse, mounted it and then rode off away from the place.

Coroner Secord and his official stenographer, Mrs. Collins, arrived at the ranch shortly before five in the morning. They were followed by Doctors Cooper of Campbell and Goder of Los Gatos who had come to carry out the autopsies. By nine that morning the jury had been impaneled. The inquest was fixed to be held at the ranch the following morning.

The autopsies completed, the bodies were removed and prepared for burial. The McDonalds and the ranch hand, Joseph, would be interred in the Hanson family plot in the Oak Hill Cemetery under the auspices of the Odd Fellows. The body of the nurse, Hisler, was taken to the house of her father on Marliere Street and would be buried separately.

Sheriff Lyndon then gave his permission for the ranch house to be cleared of debris in preparation for the inquest. But when the jury and the public who came to listen filed into the house, there had not been time to do more than clear the rubble. Many of them shivered and made nervous movements as they tried to step over the smears of blood that had dried into the wooden planks of the porch. The hearing was to be

The McDonald House and Barn

An artist's rendition of the buildings where the dreadful happenings occurred

1. *The room where Cathy and the nurse were slain.*

2. *The room where Samuel was killed.*

3. *The room where Mrs. McDonald was killed.*

4. *The point from which Leonard Ross heard the shots that finished off the Colonel.*

5. *The loft where Klaus, the hired hand, hid from Dougan.*

6. *Joseph Daniels, a hired hand, crashed through this window in an effort to escape the terrible wrath of Dougan.*

held in the dining room and those who couldn't squeeze into that room overflowed into the corridor outside.

A series of witnesses were in turn sworn in and gave various accounts which established the identities of the deceased. It was routine testimony but, as everyone there knew, it was leading up to John Dougan and what had occurred in that house. Witnesses attested to the behavior of John Dougan and his relationship with his family. There were contradictions, some said they knew the marriage to be a happy one, others that they knew there was trouble.

Mrs. Parker, a daily maid, gave evidence that Mrs. McDonald had spoken to her about Dougan saying he wanted to take his child to Mexico where he would open a saloon and see that his boy was brought up in the Catholic Church. At that, there was a ripple of whispers throughout the spectators.

Klaus, the German ranch hand, gave his version of the dreadful night; Leonard Ross, Whipple and Page theirs. The son of a Mr. Fatjo, who was a student at Santa Clara College and in the same language class as Dougan, told of how on the day before the murders Dougan was acting differently. Normally a studious person, he seemed preoccupied and continually stared into space. And, more significantly, on that day he did not take his study books home with him, as was his custom, but left them at the college.

Even Mr. Hisler, the nurse's father, provided information - - given to him second-hand by his daughter

- - that Dougan was besotted by his son and would spend hours just looking into the boy's cot.

Then Dr. Charles Cooper, one of the doctors who had performed the autopsies, stepped forward to be sworn. There was virtual silence in the room as he stood there and in a slow and deliberate voice proceeded to read his report. He spoke in lay terms so that he could be clearly understood by the jury.

The preliminaries completed, he gave the awful details.

"It was found that Colonel McDonald had been wounded five times. There was an axe wound at the outer edge of the right eye, one bullet had gone through the heart and lodged back of the seventh and eighth ribs. Another through the right lung, a third through the right shoulder, and a fourth through the right arm. The wounds were made with a .38 caliber pistol."

There was a rustling and murmuring in the crowd. The doctor continued.

"As to Mrs. McDonald, the skull was found to have been crushed and shattered. She had been struck with five blows to the head, one with the sharp edge of the axe, the other four with the blunt back of the weapon." The doctor paused to shuffle his papers.

"The nurse Hisler's skull had been crushed with the blunt edge of the axe, and there were five cuts made with the sharp edge of the axe, all of which extended to the brain."

Two women at the back of the room quickly got up from their chairs and pushed their way out into the

The Bodies of the Colonel, Stepson, Samuel, and the Ranch Hand, Joseph Daniels

Note the axe has been laid on the floor above the heads of the victims.

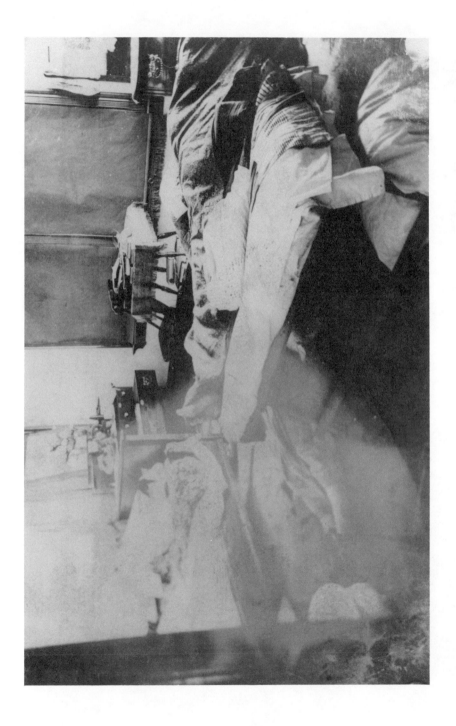

On the Bed the Dead Form of Cathy Dougan, and on the Floor, that of the Nurse

The Covered Body of Nurse Hisler Awaiting Removal

The Cabin Which Is Next to the McDonald Barn

It was out of the front door that the Colonel staggered, only to be gunned down. Joseph, the ranch hand, tried to escape by diving through the rear window. Dougan put two bullets into his back.

corridor and then to the fresh air of the porch. Other people whispered among themselves, noting the co-incidence that each victim had, peculiarly, suffered the same number of wounds.

The doctors waited for the spectators to settle down before he went on.

"Samuel McDonald was wounded five times." Here he paused as if he too placed some significance on the continued coincidence. "One bullet entered the chest, passed through the left lung, exited out the back, and imbedded itself in the floor of the room in which the victim was killed. Another bullet entered from the back, passing through the spine and lower lobe of the left lung to lodge under the skin. A third bullet went through the left shoulder and another struck the thumb of the left hand. The fifth bullet entered the left side of the jaw and passed out of the cavity of the skull just back of the right ear."

"The ranch hand, Joseph Daniels, was shot twice from the back." Here again, there were murmurs from the spectator and Coroner Secord had to call for silence. "One bullet," the doctor continued, "going through the heart, the second through the right lung and liver."

Dr. Cooper made a deep sigh and his lips tightened as he read out the final result of the examinations.

"Mrs. Dougan's death was by a lateral dislocation of the vertebrae of the neck."

Many of the women, and even a few men, were covering their faces to wipe away the tears.

The doctor concluded his evidence. "There were

finger marks on the neck, but death was produced by the head being violently twisted. There was no evidence of strangulation."

There was a stunned silence, except for the muted sounds of sobbing, when the doctor stepped back and sat down. In the cold light of day, and in the very place of the carnage, his written report delivered in unemotional tones of the deaths of six people seemed, if that were possible, even more appalling and blood chilling than all the gossip and word-of-mouth telling that had swept through the town immediately after the killings.

The coroner's jury, after being out only long enough to fill in the blank jury forms, rendered verdicts that the deceased came to their deaths at the hands of John Dougan, acting with malice aforethought.

Part 3.

THE CHASE

THE LEGEND OF JOHN DOUGAN

John Dougan arrived by the Smith's Creek Hotel at about six-thirty the following evening. The hotel was a well-known local hostelry in the foothills of Mt. Hamilton, and was patronized by travelers who had the fortitude to make the rough ride up the mountain road to the observatory at the top.

He was exhausted and hungry, and the little mare was about done in. He knew he daren't go into the hotel; word would have certainly spread this far. He would get food though; the woodchoppers' cabins in that part were often left open and empty and he had money enough to leave for whatever he took. He knew the terrain well.

His mind was clear and totally occupied by his plans, and as he turned to go up the trail by the hotel, he saw two men coming down toward him. They were on foot.

As they came closer along the trail one of the men, Everitt Snell, turned to his companion. "Oscar," he said, "That's Dougan."

"Are you sure?" Oscar Parker said.

"I am. I worked with him once. Anyway, just look at the man."

He was a sight. Face cut and swollen, clothes torn and with deep rust-colored stains all over them, and on his feet dirty wrappings of rag.

"He's probably armed," Snell said.

"Most likely," Parker said.

Dougan moved up the trail towards them and he opened his coat so that the .45, stuck into his waistband, could be plainly seen.

"Good evening," Dougan said.

The men stopped and looked up at Dougan. "Evening," they said. They saw the gun.

"Where have you come from?" Parker said. "The San Joaquin?"

Dougan hesitated. "Yes," he said. "Been up to a cabin there." He smiled. "Doing a little hunting." As he said that, he lifted his left foot as if to bring attention to the rags around it. It was a common custom for hunters in rough mountain country to wear rags over their feet; it helped with the climbing.

Dougan smiled again and touched his face. "Took a bad fall," he said.

"You look worn out," Parker said.

"Yes, that's about right.

Everitt Snell was deliberately hanging back and not talking. He didn't know if Dougan had recognized him or not and he didn't want to draw attention to himself.

Parker was trying to think fast. He didn't take to the look of that .45 Dougan had, and with what he had heard the man had done, he was nervous, and trying not to show it.

"We just come down from a longsome hike," he said. "Why don't you join us at the hotel?"

Dougan pulled on the bridle and the horse moved away from the men. He looked back at the hotel and seemed to be considering Parker's proposal.

No saddle, Snell thought. He sure must have left in a hurry. Snell went to move off down the trail. He made a play with his hand seeming to adjust his hat in an effort to shield his face from Dougan.

"Where you going?" Dougan said.

"To the hotel. I got a thirst," Snell said.

Dougan's hand moved to his waistband and Parker stiffened. They wouldn't have much of a chance with him above them on a horse.

But Dougan seemed to have second thoughts and he put his hand back up again.

"Come down with us," Parker said. "Sure you could use a drink and some food, too."

Snell was getting well down the trail now, if Parker could keep Dougan's attention, at least one of them might have a chance.

"I don't think so," Dougan said. "I have to get on. But you could tell me the best way for the San Joaquin Valley, that's where I'm heading."

"Well, take the trail and strike for the Mount Hamilton Road."

"You sure I can't go all the way by trail?"

"No," Parker said. "You have to go by the road."

Yes, take the road, Parker thought. Then it'll be easier to catch up with you.

Dougan smiled. "I'm obliged to you, sir. And thank you for your offer to dine. I best be going now."

Parker stood to the side of the trail to let him pass and as he got above him he wheeled around. "You tell that Everitt Snell, I hope he enjoys his drink," Dougan said. Then he was gone up the trail and over the rise.

Parker hurried down to the hotel. Snell was already on the telephone to the Sheriff's office.

Sheriff Ballou of San Luis Obispo Holding His
Bloodhounds, and Sheriff Lyndon to the Right

THE CHASE

❦ ❦ ❦

The evening train from San Luis Obispo brought Sheriff Ballou and his hounds. News that he was coming spread quickly and there was a crowd at the depot to meet the train. The hounds were rather small, but they were closely built and extremely active, swerving against their collars continually, as if anxious to get on their way. They were constantly sniffing the ground, and one of the men in the crowd said, "Once they get those hounds on his trail it'll be over soon enough."

When the message came from Everitt Snell, Sheriff Lyndon quickly decided to move the dogs and the bulk of his men to Smith's Creek. He would set up a headquarters at the hotel.

"This is the first solid lead we've had yet," he told the newspaper reporters who were now almost part of his growing retinue. "I'm confident we shall apprehend the murderer."

Sheriff Lyndon's reputation as a tireless, confident investigator had grown hourly, it seemed, and it continued to grow in spite of one restless, empty-handed day following the next. A photograph, a tin type, actually, that had been overlooked by Dougan in his search at the ranch, had been turned into a wanted poster on the Sheriff's orders and was being circulated throughout California. Hundreds of men, all fully armed, congregated in Smith's Creek, eager to join the man hunt.

As it turned out, the much heralded hound dogs were unable to demonstrate their animal cunning and ability. Early that morning a hail storm in the mountains, coupled with dense fogs, hampered and inhibited their special talents. They were returned to Campbell to await further developments.

When the fogs did clear and the men were able to mount up to continue the chase, there came a shout from a gully just over the rise where Parker had last seen Dougan.

"Over here," the voice called out.

Sheriff Lyndon and his men hurried up the trail.

The man was standing in the gully and next to him, tethered to a tree, was a small mare. It was munching on the grass.

"That's his horse," Everitt Snell said.

"You sure?" the Sheriff said.

"I'm sure. Ask Parker if you want another opinion."

"He must have gone on foot," the Sheriff said. "He can't be far ahead; the hail and fog would have slowed him just like us. I want every gulch, every rise and every arroyo searched. Leave nothing to chance."

Search they did but there continued to be no further sign of John Dougan. It was a weary band that camped out that night. Some sprawled asleep around the campfires, others eating and drinking endless cups of coffee; all of them dog tired.

Not many bothered to lift a head when the sound of a horse was heard and the rider came into the camp.

Seth Churchhill, an Old-Time Scout
on Dougan's Trail

It was the newspaper reporter. He tethered the horse and walked over to the lone figure of Sheriff Lyndon, who was keeping to himself and leaning with his back against a tree studying a map by the light of the campfires.

"Evenin' Sheriff. Mind if I join you?"

The Sheriff looked up from the map.

"Go ahead," he said.

The reporter lay out on the damp ground and took a Mexican cigarillo from his pocket and lit up to enjoy a smoke. He surveyed the scene: the men dark shapeless figures in the flickering, warm, light from the fires. Shuffling sounds when one of them shifted to find a more comfortable spot and the smell of horses and bacon and beans and coffee with smoke from pipes and cigarillos.

"No luck?"

"No," the Sheriff said.

"I heard about the horse being found."

"Yeah."

"No other signs?"

"He broke into a cabin. Took some food, it seemed, and I guess a pair of boots."

"He can't be far then?"

"Don't reckon so."

Sheriff Lyndon handed the reporter a mug.

"Pour yourself some coffee."

The reporter went to the fire and sat on his haunches to pour some of the black coffee from the pot that was suspended above the glowing embers, then he was back by the Sheriff organizing the placement of the coffee cup on the ground, next to his notebook. His pencil was in hand at the ready.

"They had the service for the family at Oak Hill Cemetery today. Odd Fellows handled it. Buried 'em in the Hanson family plot, even Joseph, the hand," the Sheriff told him.

"What about the Hisler woman?" the reporter said.

"Her father took care of that. He's a broken man."

"Yeah, she was all he had, wife went some years ago."

"I wouldn't want to be Dougan if Hisler ever got to him before any of us," the Sheriff said.

"You think that could be likely?"

The reporter's pencil was poised over the note pad.

"Anything would be likely if you want to know the truth."

"What would your opinion be about John Dougan, that a man could do such a terrible deed?"

The Sheriff gave thought before he answered. "Sometimes a man gets driven to do things no sane man would contemplate."

The Citizens' Executive Committee, consisting of leading members of the Campbell Town Council, called a mass meeting at the courthouse. The meeting was given over to outlining ways and means for raising a $10,000 reward. The first decision was to print and issue a poster. Above a large head and shoulders picture of John Dougan was the headline. Under the picture followed details of the crime and then a description of Dougan.

"We cannot say how many of these posters we will

THE LEGEND OF JOHN DOUGAN

M U R D E R !

TEN THOUSAND DOLLARS REWARD

To be paid by the citizens of Santa Clara County, California
DEAD or ALIVE
One thousand dollars reward will be paid
by the Governor of California
For the Arrest and Convinction of JOHN DOUGAN

DESCRIPTION

Twenty-seven years old. Six feet high. About 165 pounds.
Has sharp features, dark hair and mustache, blue eyes,
medium complexion. When last seen he wore a blacksuit,
cutaway coat and black soft hat. He walks very erect,
chin recedes when he laughs.

issue," the chairman of the committee told the newspapers. "But we intend to flood the country with them. Every post office on the Pacific Coast, every police officer, every railroad station, hotel and restaurant will be given one."

A circular was issued by the ladies' sub-committee in an effort to enlist the help of as many women as possible. The circular started off by saying, "Dear Madam, For the first time in the history of this State women are appealed to in a cause the like of which they have never before been asked to aid.

"Three of your sex have been most cruelly murdered, and we desire the material assistance of every woman in bringing the murderer, John Dougan, to justice."

A main purpose of all this activity, one of the ladies said, was to try to ensure that Dougan's face would be familiar to as many people as possible so that, should he be seen or ask for help, he would be known.

"We are determined that the fiend be captured," the lady said.

In spite of the days going by without any sign of Dougan being caught, the enthusiasm of the people of Campbell for his capture never abated. They even tolerated the presence in town of the professional gunfighters and bounty hunters the posted reward had attracted.

Stories started to filter down from the mountain ranches where the mail was only occasionally delivered from Evergreen and Madrone, and usually brought by one of the ranchers of the neighborhood

The Rural Free Mail Delivery

who chanced by the post office.

It was not surprising therefore that none of the residents knew of the terrible event that had taken place in Campbell Station until one Sunday morning the rural free mail delivery arrived, containing a copy of the *Mercury*. Charles Coe, the owner of the Coe ranch, was astounded to read about John Dougan, whom he had seen only the previous Friday.

As Coe told his story, Dougan was well known to him, having worked some years ago on his land. That Friday he looked like he was worn out from a hard tramp through the brush. His face was scratched and he spoke of being hungry.

Dougan talked of making his way in the direction of Packwood Valley, south of Smith's Creek, Coe said.

After Dougan had left, Coe thought the circumstances of his visit rather strange. The mystery was cleared up on the delivery of the newspaper, and immediately after reading the account Coe sent word to all his neighbors. Others then recounted stories of Dougan either calling for food or having been seen. The reward no doubt giving fuel to their memories.

After learning that Dougan had been seen in the mountain region, a rancher by the name of Wadhams began an investigation of his own and told of finding fresh footprints of a man upon old trails where men seldom go on foot or even horseback.

The tracks were not regular, and some of them were blurred as if made by a man who had wrapped his feet with rags. They were so uncertain and occasional on the trails that Wadhams could not be sure whether the man had both feet covered at times and at other times had worn his shoes. Besides the footprints there were strange marks on some of the trails.

Later it was shown that the marks proved almost beyond doubt to be made by a bicycle that was sometimes carried and sometimes pushed along over trails where it was too steep and rough to ride.

The sight and knowledge brought to Wadhams' mind, he reported, that on the previous Friday night at around midnight, when he was on his way home from a dance in the San Felipe school house and was crossing the bridge by bright moonlight, he saw tracks which looked freshly made. He reasoned that the rider had passed that way recently, perhaps on his way to Hollister via the rough wagon road that the ranchers used in going to that town. The road, as is well known, is used for the procuring of supplies from Gilroy by way of Madrone.

But, still no trace of the bicycle was found and how the tracks from its wheels got that high on such rough terrain could not be explained.

Sheriff McEvoy and Under Sheriff Mansfield, both of San Mateo county, who were considered experts in the sport of wheeling, could lend no opinion, other than Dougan might have had a confederate waiting on the upper reaches of the mountain with his bicycle.

Whatever the answer might have been, the report was one of many that circulated.

It almost went unnoticed among the never ending flood of news and gossip that George Dougan had successfully applied for the adoption of his brother's only child. Similarly, the publishing of Mrs. McDonald's will aroused no particular interest in spite of the fact that it perhaps contained a small but telling confirmation of the situation that existed in her family. Mrs. McDonald's orchard property had been valued at $30,000; it brought in an annual income of $1,500. It was left in its entirety to her son, Samuel. Cathy, the wife of John Dougan, the will stated, was bequeathed - - maybe surprisingly - - a meager $100. The will was dated March 7, 1896. It revoked all previous wills; everything though, by the rule of consanguinity, went to John Dougan, Jr.

Reports from around the state arrived almost weekly announcing that John Dougan had been apprehended. All proved to be groundless, and many a man spent a rough night in jail awaiting confirmation of his true identity. Theories about Dougan's whereabouts proliferated: some suggested he had been seen in Cuba, others that he was working in a mine somewhere in Mexico. The most prevelant thought was that, in his despair at the realization of his terrible crimes, he had committed suicide.

More by chance than design, a group of men, all of whom had some close connection to Dougan, happened to come gathered in the Belloli Saloon one July afternoon.

William Goring was the first there. A cohort from the cycling club, he was an old friend when they would all gather and the talk would be of trails and maps and times it took to get from here to there and back again.

He thought back over conversations he'd had with Dougan and tried to put himself in his place. A good man most would say, certainly not one prone to violence. How though would any of them have reacted in the same circumstance, he thought? Surely not in the same vicious manner, that was for sure. But then who's to know how you would react, given the same situation?

Shelly, from the Warwick Cyclery, came in then. He could see Goring way through to the back of the place, so he went in to join him.

"Afternoon, Bill," he said.

"Hello, Shelly. How's your bicycle business?"

"Well, since you should ask, ever since Dougan went crazy it's been great. Seems like everyone wants to get on wheels and go touring the mountains. Not many up to it, though."

"He was a strong man."

"Mind if I join you?" The man was tall and thin and he wore cowboy clothes. He carried a Winchester rifle. Both men knew him and Goring pulled back a chair.

"What will you drink Trace?" he said.

"Beer, a beer would be fine."

"Still at it?" Shelly said.

"Yep. That Lyndon don't want to give up. But I reckon we must have searched this entire area fifty times by now."

The waiter came up to the table and took the order. They were all drinking beer.

"Got any leads?" Goring said.

"Sure we got all the leads you could want an' then some. God it seems like everybody in this state and beyond has seen the man. Even as far as Nevada they seen him."

"It's that reward money," Shelly said. "Wouldn't mind it myself, come to think of it."

"Talking of Dougan, isn't that George comin' in?" Shelly said.

The other two turned their heads. "Yeah that's him," Goring said, and he stood up and went back down the bar to where George Dougan was standing. "George, you want to join us at the back?"

George Dougan was surprised, but when he saw who it was, he smiled. "Yeah, I would, Bill, beats standing up here on my own."

They all knew each other and soon they were having a little drinking party. Nothing boisterous, just a few drinks, enough to get them talking freely.

"Haven't seen you in town, George not for some time."

"Well, you know I don't feel I'd be too welcome, it seems to me."

"Hear you got yourself married off," Shelly said.

"Yeah, I did. A good woman she is - - and mother."

There was a short silence. "How is that boy?" Goring said.

"He's real good. Good little fellow."

Trace wiped the beer from his moustache and then

rubbed his big, long fingered hand over his chin. "What you reckon to do, George? I mean you going to be staying in San Jose or what?"

They were all looking at George, waiting for his answer.

"No. We're going to be moving, that's for sure. Back east, maybe, or perhaps south. I haven't quite made up my mind as yet." He took a big swig at his beer. "Came to the bank today. To see about moving John Jr.'s money. He's got a tidy sum after they sold off that ranch."

"Wouldn't have bought the place myself," Shelly said. "Even if I'd had the money."

The waiter brought another round of drinks. He wished they had gone on talking while he was serving; he knew George Dougan by sight and the others. Might have picked up some good piece of talk, but they waited until he was through.

"What you think about John?" Goring said. "I mean, you think he's gone, or what?"

"I don't know anymore than you do, Bill. One thing is sure enough, he wouldn't have killed himself, not John."

"Why you say that?" Trace said.

"Cause he was a good Catholic, better than I ever was, and Catholics don't do that. That's the worst thing a Catholic could ever do, Trace, take his own life. That's a mortal sin."

"Sure was peculiar," Shelly said.

"What was?" George said.

"About that bicycle. You know he came in just a

few days before - - and he was set to fit it up like he was going a long ways."

"They never did find it," Trace said. "Searched every which way."

"Think that's what he's done?" Goring said.

"I don't know," Trace said. "All I know is that we found that mare where he left it, but we never found any bicycle. There was talk about tracks up in the mountains, and sure enough could have been Dougan. But who's to know?"

"He could have done it, if you ask me," Shelly said. "He was strong, I mean very strong, on a pair of wheels."

"According to Parker, he was heading to the San Joaquin Valley. Told him to take the Mt. Hamilton Road."

"Listen, Trace," Goring said. "One thing I know about John Dougan, he wouldn't have to ask no one the way to the San Joaquin. Christ, he knew those trails better than any of us."

He paused and lifted his glass and drank the beer. "Mexico, I would say, heard him talk about Mexico. Take his boy down there where he could be brought up a Catholic and nobody would argue with him. That was what kept John Dougan's steam up, his boy being a Catholic. Ain't that right, George?"

George Dougan downed the last of his beer. "You may have said a truth there Bill," he said. "John certainly was serious where that was concerned."

He stood up. "I have to go," he said. He stood up and offered his hand to the three men and each one took it in turn around the table.

"Think maybe we'll see you again, George?" Goring said.

"No, I think not, Bill. We'll be moving on very soon now. Who knows - - might even change a name or two - - got to think of the boy and him growing up."

"Maybe, for old times sake, you'll keep in touch," Goring said.

"I'll try, Bill," George said. "I really will."

All of a sudden they were a sad bunch of men. And they stood up as George Dougan left the place.

Part 4.

TWELVE YEARS LATER

THE LEGEND OF JOHN DOUGAN

Whatever age a man is, twelve years is a long time. But if he is young, then it is forever; older, and he wonders where it went. Either way, twelve years is supposed to be twelve years. Time, though, does seem to alter depending on where you stand in your life.

Twelve years in Campbell Station was like any-where else. Kids were gangly and trouble most of the time, young boys had grown to young men, and the older ones, who remembered first hand, told the story of the McDonald family and pointed to the posters that were still displayed. Some made up the story to be more than it was, although what more could it really be? Anyway, their part in it. Perhaps they stretched things a bit and said they were there just after it happened, or that they thought they might have been the next victim. However it was told, John Dougan was a mystery - - or rather where he went and what happened to him was the mystery.

The town had grown; there were new buildings and new people on the city council. Old man Campbell had gone, new thoughts had come with new people, and the American Protective Association had passed into obscurity.

But when men met in the saloon, or at a barbecue party, eventually the talk would come around to long tales of John Dougan. How he was a beast, a raving lunatic, or how he was driven to it by that family and the wife who had turned on him. That some trigger in his brain went bad and fired off a madness that was alien to the man his friends knew and admired.

They would wonder about him and what had happened to the boy who had inherited all that McDonald money. Names were changed, some said, and the family moved back East. Who wouldn't change a name with a history like theirs? Who would want to burden a boy who slept through the most terrible night there would be with tales told him about a murdering father? Better arrange things so that it could never be, and if he ever did chance to hear about it, then he would think it was some other family - - not his.

On December 1, 1908, there appeared in the San Jose newspaper a wanted poster with a picture of John Dougan and the year it was taken, 1895, scratched on it. Right across the top was printed in bold letters, "ARREST FOR MURDER. DEAD OR ALIVE." Then there followed much of the original poster's words that had appeared twelve years ago. In fact the last paragraph of the top part of the poster finished by saying, "The above is a revision of the circular sent out by J.H. Lyndon, Sheriff of this county at the time of the murder. I waive all claims to the reward. Wire information at my expense." It was signed Arthur B. Langsford, Sheriff of Santa Clara County, San Jose, California.

Underneath there came a second heading, "ADDITIONAL DESCRIPTION OF JOHN DOUGAN. As he was in 1896." This was in great length and came with headings followed by descriptions in detail; height, weight, hair, eyes, nose, mustache, mouth, teeth, chin, neck, hands, thumbs,

John Dougan, Fugitive
The picture used throughout the United States for every DEAD OR ALIVE poster printed. It was made from the wedding photograph of John Dougan and his wife, Cathy.

feet and finally scars: "When a boy cut left foot with axe; this is said to have left a big scar, running from left side of instep to outside of foot under left ankle."

The poster continued, "If you are satisfied you have the right man located, arrest and send me photographs, with and without hat on, with complete description, height, weight, marks, scars, etc., also samples of writing if possible. So many have mistakenly thought they had this man spotted, and so many of our officers have had to make useless trips, that I must refuse to make any trips outside of the State until I am positive you have the right man."

There then came a specimen of handwriting said to be that of John Dougan. It appeared to be only part of a document and in all probability written to his then wife. The style of writing was that of an educated person. It said, "...valley on the mountain sides are immense boulders as large as a small house and some considerably smaller. I have to go to collect a . . . Good night love."

So when, right after publication of the poster, word came that a man from Missouri said to be John Dougan himself was coming in on a train, well, it was understandable that the whole town was in a frenzy of excitement about such an event. This time, they said, it was certain - - this was THE John Dougan, not some imposter. The real John Dougan, murderer, was coming in on the noon train. Pity Sheriff Lyndon was not there to see the sight, after all he had done.

Nearly the whole town, it seemed, turned out to

meet that noontime train. It was forty minutes late, which kept them all on a sharp, nervous edge of anticipation. The other passengers on that train wondered what all the commotion was about and some of them hesitated to inquire, others even waited to see this famous murderer disembark from the train they themselves had travelled on. That would be another story to tell at some future date. How they had been on the same train that brought the infamous John Dougan home to roost.

How would he look after twelve years? With a beard, perhaps, or clean shaven, without that majestic moustache he used to sport? Well, it wouldn't be long till they found out, there was a party getting off at the far end of the train. A group of men, most of them obviously sheriffs or deputies and one of them just standing there doing what they told him to do.

They walked on each side of him and two more behind. He was taller than all of them, except one. They hadn't put shackles on him and from the way they were armed - - two of the men were carrying Winchesters - - there was probably no need. The man was clean shaven, and his face had the look of someone from the outdoors. The deputies from Campbell had formed a line to keep back the crowd who had come to see the man, but it was pressing forward as the group came down the platform towards it.

Now that he was closer you could see his hair was well salted with grey, and if the posters were anything to go by he had put on some weight. He sure weighed

169

more than 165 pounds. A couple of women were even carrying copies of the old poster and they kept looking at it, then back up at the man. Yeah, he had blue eyes all right, but they weren't so certain you could call his features sharp. Twelve years older, though; time can make a difference in things like that.

The Campbell deputies made a corridor through the crowd so that the party could pass. Surprisingly, the crowd was quiet; it seemed as if all of them were concentrating so hard looking at the man they said was John Dougan that there was no energy left over for shouting out at him. Then he was gone, on his way to the new courthouse. The odd thing, most of them thought, was that he didn't act like a criminal or even as if he were afraid. No, that man they brought off the train was smiling.

"All right, Dougan," the Sheriff said.

"The name is Eli Kroll," the man said. "I do keep telling you that. And I do it, sir, because that's my rightful name."

"Oh yeah? Well, as far as we all here are concerned, you are John Dougan until someone proves otherwise."

Eli Kroll sighed. "You've got my papers, Sheriff, and they all say Kroll."

"Papers - - what do papers prove?"

"As I keep saying, Sheriff, they prove who I am."

"All they prove, boy," one of the deputies said, "is that they are paper! It don't mean that's you there in those papers. Why, could be me, if I had a mind to call myself Eli Kroll."

"What were you doing in Nevada, Dougan?" the Sheriff said.

The man calling himself Eli Kroll smiled. "Just what I told the deputies, Sheriff. I was visiting."

"You were a long ways from home."

"Yes, sir, I was."

"Torsen," the Sheriff said to one of the deputies. "Take him downstairs and find him a cell. We'll talk again, Dougan," he said to the man.

So they took the man away and put him in a cell. In their records they noted that a John Dougan had been booked.

"We got to have an identification parade, Mr. Mayor," the Sheriff said.

The mayor nodded his head. "How close are you sailing to the wind, Jess?" he said.

The Sheriff leaned back in his chair. "Pretty close, I reckon."

"Your boys just took him out of Nevada. No legal papers or anything?"

"They got him in Carson City, Mr. Mayor. He was headed up to the pass. They just helped him on his journey into the California."

"If he turns out to be the wrong man - - again - - then you might just be in a little trouble."

"He's Dougan; on my badge, that man is John Dougan."

Nobody could keep a story like that to themselves and it wasn't long before the word had gotten around town about how the man from Missouri came to be sitting in a cell in the courthouse.

It seems someone in Carson City, who used to live in Campbell Station, recognized the man as he was sitting in a hotel dining room having a meal. This man checked with the hotel desk clerk and together they looked at the register which showed that the man was called Eli Kroll and came from a town in Missouri. "That's a phony name," the man said. "Why, I used to see John Dougan when he worked in the Campbell bank, and that man sitting in there eating his dinner is the same."

So a telephone call was made to the sheriff in Campbell and a party of deputies left immediately.

"Wonder what he's up to in Carson," the man said. The desk clerk said that Kroll had told him he was visiting and then would be moving on in a couple of days to see a relative in California. Least that's what he told him.

The man calling himself Eli Kroll sat in the cell and wondered what they would do next. All they really had to do was make a telephone call to his town in Missouri or send a telegraph and that should be the end of it. The trouble was, he figured, that they were so riled up and sure he was John Dougan that maybe they wouldn't bother to try to prove themselves wrong. Then anything could happen and it would be too late.

Surely he was entitled to make a call himself? If they would just let him do that, then he could clear it up and be out of there. Over the years, he had heard, there had been many such cases of mistaken identity.

He just hoped this would be another one.

One night in jail wouldn't be too bad - - he could take that - - just so it was one night.

The following morning the Sheriff and the mayor met with the City Council and they discussed what should be done. One of the council members said he had read about back East they were using some-thing called fingerprinting to establish identity. The Sheriff said that was right, but what could that prove in this case? They didn't have any fingerprints of John Dougan on record - - they weren't fingerprint-ing in Campbell back in 1896 and so there was nothing could be proved.

"We can't hold this man here for long," the mayor said. "Not without proof. He can't be held on the say so of one man, and that's for sure."

"I reckon the first thing that's got to be done," a council member said, "is to check out his story."

"I already sent a telegraph to the sheriff in Missouri in the town he says he's from," the Sheriff said. "But it might take a day or two to get a reply."

"And what about his handwriting, have you checked that?"

The Sheriff's face took on a smug look. "I have," he said and he took, with something of a flourish, a piece of paper from his inside jacket pocket. "Perhaps you would be good enough to pass that around the table," he said.

They each studied the paper and the handwriting that was written on it which said, "Across the valley and into the mountains."

The mayor smiled, "Nearly some of the same wording as on your poster, I see, Sheriff."

The Sheriff nodded and was pleased with himself.

"From what I remember," a council member said, "isn't there a different slant to this writing style?"

The Sheriff was not pleased. "That may be true but any man would take pains to alter his writing should he consider it was to come under scrutiny. I am convinced we have our man and can prove it."

"Supposing it all checks out," the mayor said. "But only back twelve years? What then?"

"Claims he's got a family there. Wife and two kids," the Sheriff said.

"How old are they?" a councilman said. There was an urgency in his voice.

"That's the thing. Twins, a twelve-year-old-girl and boy."

There was silence in the room. "That would be too much to consider," a councilman said.

"Maybe," the Sheriff said.

"Wasn't the boy adopted by his brother George?" the mayor said.

"Yeah. But nobody knows where George Dougan went when he left San Jose. Maybe he went to Missouri, too."

"Sheriff," the mayor said, and his voice was testy. "Just let's check some facts here."

"Tell you what I want to do," the Sheriff said. "I want to have an identification. There's plenty of people in this town knew John Dougan. Let 'em take a look at him. Then in a day or two, we'll have a reply from Missouri. Either way we'll have more to go on."

"Supposing he is identified," the mayor said. "And the Missouri people say this Kroll has only been there twelve years. What then?"

"Then I guess we have to take him back and make it positive - - if we can get him out of town alive."

The man, Eli Kroll, readily agreed with the Sheriff to an identification parade. "Best thing," he said. "I know I'm not this man, Dougan."

"Yeah, well maybe we'll find out for sure," the Sheriff said.

A notice was posted outside the courthouse and it spread the news quickly enough.

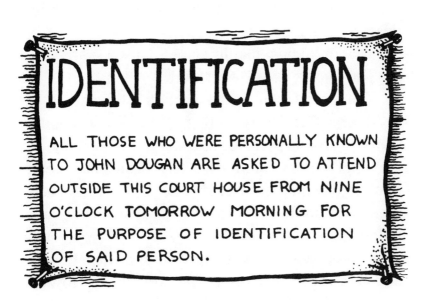

IDENTIFICATION

ALL THOSE WHO WERE PERSONALLY KNOWN TO JOHN DOUGAN ARE ASKED TO ATTEND OUTSIDE THIS COURT HOUSE FROM NINE O'CLOCK TOMORROW MORNING FOR THE PURPOSE OF IDENTIFICATION OF SAID PERSON.

A defense lawyer might very well have argued that the wording, as it was drawn up by the Sheriff, was one-sided. But as there was no defense lawyer, yet, that was academic.

The Sheriff assigned two deputies to escort the man and to stand with him as the people filed in front of him. A platform had been erected at the foot of the courthouse steps, and at five minutes to nine, the courthouse doors opened and the two deputies walked out, one on each side of the man.

Torsen, one of the deputies, didn't like it.

"This is no way to treat any man," he said to his colleague, a man called Ayer. "I don't care what he's done. To make him stand on a soap box and be stared at."

"He killed a whole family," Ayer said. "All he deserves is a rope."

"We don't know that for sure," Torsen said.

"The Sheriff does," Ayer said.

"The Sheriff is up for re-election," Torsen said.

At first there were only a dozen or so people standing around in small groups as the deputies stood the man on the platform. His hands had been manacled behind his back, but he stood upright and there was a smile on his face as if he didn't have a care in the world.

Two women detached themselves from their friends and walked over to the box. Their friends tried to hide the grins on their faces as they watched.

"Morning, Mr. Dougan," one of the women said.

The man smiled at her. "My name is Eli Kroll,

ma'am."

The women looked at each other, then back at the man.

The second woman said, "I want to ask you a question."

"Ask away," the man said.

"Whatever happened to the money from that fore-closure on the Penn property of yours?"

"I don't know any Penn, ma'am. And the only property I ever owned is back in Missouri."

"What do you say, ladies?" Deputy Ayer said. "Is this Dougan or not?"

"We worked in the bank with him," one of the women said.

"He sure looks like him," the other woman said.

Deputy Ayer handed the women an open book. "Just sign your names and put an X against whichever you think."

The book had columns ruled in it with the headings: Name, Yes, and No.

The first woman signed her name and she looked up at the man again, studied his face, then she wrote an X in the Yes column. She handed the book to her friend and her friend didn't even bother to look up at the man, she just signed her name and wrote her X in the Yes column.

By this time a crowd was beginning to form.

All during the morning, people would file by in front of the man, some would ask questions, which the man would try to answer, but he never agreed with anything that could at all connect him with John

Dougan. The columns in the book quickly began to fill. When Deputy Torsen looked at the pages he counted the X's about even. Not what the Sheriff wanted, he thought.

At noon, Deputy Ayer called out to the crowd, "We have to take him back in for food and drink."

There were murmurs in the crowd as the three men went up the courthouse steps and through the door. "Sure as hell looks like him to me," a man said.

"Difficult to tell," another said. "Wouldn't want to put my say-so on the wrong man."

"Twelve years is a long time, you can forget how a man looked," a woman said.

"Beats me how he can stand there smiling all the time," a man said. "I sure wouldn't feel like smiling in his position, and standing on a soap box for everyone to see."

By late afternoon the smile on the face of the man called Eli Kroll was beginning to fade. The sun was still hot and standing there with no hat on - - the Sheriff wouldn't allow him to wear one - - he was feeling weary.

Seemed to him like the entire town had turned out during the day. A lot of people must have known John Dougan judging by the numbers who had put their names in the book.

At four o'clock that afternoon, Father O'Reilly and the man called Trace walked into the town square together. Trace well remembered the Dougan he had talked with many times over a glass of beer in the saloon.

They stood at the back of the crowd and watched. At first, neither of them said anything, they were too intent at studying the man on the platform. "It's a dreadful thing," Father O'Reilly said.

"Yes, it is," Trace said. "What do you think, though?"

"I can't be certain. I'll have to talk to him, hear his voice. But he does look like John Dougan, sure enough."

"Do you want to go up now?" Trace said.

The priest sighed. "I suppose we have to, Trace."

They made their way through the crowd, and many of the people there recognized them and the crowd became quiet as the two men stood in front of the man who had his hands manacled behind his back.

"John?" Trace said.

"Eli," the man said.

"It's been a long time, some years," Trace said.

"A long day for me," the man said.

Trace was searching his memory for things to say that only he and John Dougan would know about and all the while he kept his eyes on his face. Looking into his eyes with each question, not really hearing the answers but trying to see some flicker that would tell him more than words. Then the realization that even though you could never forget a friend, the years and their special circumstances surely affected a judgment.

"Would you swear by almighty God?" the priest said.

"Yes, I would," the man said.

"Then are you John Dougan?"

The man looked down at the priest, looked directly at him.

"I swear my name is Eli Kroll."

The priest stepped forward and took the book from Deputy Ayer. He signed his name, and he looked up at the man once again. Then he made his X. He handed the book to Trace and Trace looked down at the pages. Father O'Reilly's name was plain to see, so was his X, under the Yes column.

Trace handed the book back to the deputy. "I can't be sure yet," he said. "I'll come back."

As the two men left, the crowd began to get restless. "What did he say?" a man called out. "Yeah, what did he say?" another said.

Deputy Ayer looked across at Torsen and he smiled.

"You shouldn't tell them," Torsen said.

"What the hell, they'll know sooner or later," Ayer said.

"His own priest said yes," Ayer told the crowd.

There was a roar from the crowd. "His own priest identified him," one of them called out. "Yeah, that's the murderer Dougan," said another.

An old man pushed his way through the crowd and whispers went up. "That's Hisler, father of the murdered nurse."

The old man, Hisler, went right up to the platform. Tears were beginning to come to his eyes, and in a low voice that could be hardly heard, he said, "Murderer," and he spat at the man. Tried to spit right in his face, but because of the height of the platform, the spit didn't reach up that far, and in his frustration the old man began to hit out and as he punched he kept crying out, "Murderer, filthy murderer."

Deputy Torsen moved quickly in front of the man and he held Hisler back. "That's enough of that," he said.

The crowd caught the new mood and they started to chant, "Mur-der-er, mur-der-er."

Torsen turned back to Ayer. "We'd better get him out of here," he said. "There's going to be trouble."

Then what Torsen feared all along happened. Somebody at the back of the crowd yelled it out, loud and clear. "Lynch him."

The courthouse door opened and the Sheriff stood at the top of the steps. "Get him back up here," he called out. The deputies began to go back up the courthouse steps, and in their haste the man tripped. The crowd let out another roar as he fell backwards, and the deputies more or less had to drag him up the steps.

The crowd was like a wave of rats advancing on a prey. As the deputies and the man retreated, so they scampered up towards them.

Torsen cocked his Winchester and stood his ground. "That's far enough," he cried out. "Right there, just stop right there."

It worked, and gave Ayer and the man time to reach the courthouse door. Torsen, with his Winchester held out in front of him, followed them through the door and then it was locked.

"That's a mad bunch," Torsen said.

"You don't forget in a hurry what this man did," Ayer said.

"I didn't do anything," the man called Eli Kroll cried out. "I've never been here before, don't you understand that? Never even been in this place before." His voice was shrill and afraid.

"Take him downstairs," the Sheriff said.

When they had taken the man down to the cells, the sheriff turned to the door and unlocked it. Then he went outside and stood on the top of the steps. He held up his arms for silence.

"Listen. Everybody just calm down and we'll get on with this."

"Lynch the murderer," someone yelled out.

The square was filled with people and for the first time he began to worry if he could control what might happen. He'd seen lynch parties before and they always started out this way - - a crowd and a few local hardnecks who fired them up - - then things got really ugly.

"This has gotta be done legal," he shouted to them.

"Then lynch him legal."

"Yeah, yeah," they roared.

It wasn't going to be any good. They were in no mood to listen. As he turned to go back inside the door he heard them coming up the steps behind him. He nearly tripped on the steps himself as he hurried to get back inside the door.

"Close it," he cried out. "Close the damn door."

He got inside before the first body hit. "Help me bar this goddamn thing," he said. It took six of them to force the door closed and put the bars up. As they relaxed, they could hear they crowd outside; they were crashing their fists on the door.

"Think it'll hold?" one of them said.

"It better," the Sheriff said.

❦ ❦ ❦

When Trace had walked away from the courthouse with Father O'Reilly, he had asked him why he had been so certain that the man was Dougan.

"He didn't swear he wasn't," the priest said. "He only swore his name was Eli Kroll. That wasn't enough for me."

"You could have damned the man," Trace said.

"I know. I think it was the most difficult decision I have ever made in my life. They could lynch him, you know."

"Yes," Trace said. "They're in the mood, too."

"And what about you?" the priest said.

"I couldn't be sure. I'd known John Dougan a long time, off and on, Father. Even so, after twelve years, it's difficult and there are many things to consider."

"Would you have marked *yes* even if you were sure he was Dougan?" the priest said.

"I really don't know, Father. I can't hold with what he did, but you get torn between things. And if that man up there is not John Dougan, then I might think he could become the seventh victim if I said yes and it was wrong."

The priest shook his head. "You know, he seemed so familiar to me, not just the physical look of him. His voice, his manner, and the way he stood there smiling. Something very familiar."

"Maybe you're right, Father. I'll have to think more about it. I'll have to be sure."

"Trace, right or wrong, your decision may make no difference at all. Although, may God forgive me, I think mine may have done."

When the train came in the following morning, there was only one passenger who got off - - a woman. There was no one to meet her and her luggage consisted of only a single piece, a small brown leather bag. She stood alone on the platform, just she and the train, and then the train was gone.

She was about thirty-five - - maybe more - - and well built. Light brown hair and a good face without too much make-up. She seemed in charge of herself, confident. If a person looked closely at her, he might discern a certain heavy sophistication in her face, and in her carriage too.

She walked slowly down the platform. As she checked her ticket she asked the station master how far it was to the courthouse. He was very solicitous and immediately ordered a surrey to take her there.

"There's a commotion going on," he told her.

"Oh really," the woman said, and she appeared unconcerned.

When they reached the courthouse, the woman stepped from the surrey and paid off the driver. The waiting crowd there watched her - - there was little else to watch - - and studied her as she went up the steps to the courthouse door. She knocked on the door and waited. A voice sounded out. "Who's there?"

"I have come to see Eli Kroll," she said.

"Oh, yeah," the voice said.

"Yes."

There was a pause as if the person on the other side of the door realized this was not a townsperson trying to gain entrance.

The crowd in the square, which had diminished overnight, was curious about this stranger who had seemed so poised.

"Who wants to see him?" the voice said.

"This is Mrs. Eli Kroll," the woman said, and a tremor seemed to go through the crowd.

There was another pause and then she heard the bars being drawn and the door being unlocked. Deputy Torsen stood there. "Did you say Mrs. Eli Kroll?"

"I did," she said.

The door was opened fully and the woman was allowed through. Once she was inside, the Sheriff was hastily called to come from the meeting where a discussion was in progress to evaluate the telegrapher's reply received that morning from Missouri.

"You say you are Mrs. Kroll?" the Sheriff said.

"Yes, I do," she said.

"Can you prove it?"

"Of course."

She handed the Sheriff a sheaf of papers, including her marriage certificate and various other documents. The Sheriff studied them and then, almost reluctantly, returned them to the woman.

"Okay, Mrs. Kroll. What do you want?"

"What was that?" she said.

"I said, what do want?"

"My husband, what else?" the woman said.

"We have your husband here on suspicion," the Sheriff said.

"Suspicion of what?"

"Murder."

"That is ridiculous," the woman said.

The Sheriff was not used to being spoken to like that, and certainly not by a woman. "Would you take a seat, ma'am," he said. "I have some details to take care of."

"Not for long, I hope, Sheriff," she said.

"Torsen," the Sheriff said. "Take care of this lady."

"The name is Kroll, Mrs. Eli Kroll," she said to Torsen, and the deputy smiled. "Yes, ma'am, I know."

"This way, Mrs. Kroll," he said, and he took her to the waiting room.

The Sheriff hurried back to the meeting.

"What was it, Sheriff?" the mayor said.

"A woman who says who says she is Kroll's wife. Must have come in on the morning train." There was a hush in that room, broken only by the sudden intakes of breath by the members of the committee.

"Can she prove it?" a councilman said.

"Has all the right looking papers," the Sheriff said. "Marriage certificate says Caroline Kroll."

"Give me the telegraph message again," the mayor said.

The Sheriff passed the paper across the desk and the mayor studied it, reading it over for probably the fourth time.

The report was terse and written in the shorthand style adopted for such messages. It confirmed the existence of an Eli Kroll, his wife Caroline, and two twin children, aged twelve. Resident for ten years, it said, the family having moved there from the state of Ohio. The message concluded by stating the family was in excellent standing and that, in fact, Eli Kroll was himself a member of the town council.

The mayor put the telegraph form down on the table. "While you were out of the room, Sheriff, we were talking about checking further, with the people in Ohio. But now, I don't know, with this latest development."

"I don't think our position is tenable, Mr. Mayor," a councilmen said. "Half the town says the man is Dougan, the other half not. And now we have the man's wife and that message . . ." His voice trailed off.

"There's no proof," the Sheriff said. "It could be a put-up job."

"There's no proof either way, Sheriff," the mayor said.

"Why don't we ask this Mrs. Kroll in here," a

councilman said. "Perhaps she could make up our minds for us."

❦ ❦ ❦

Mrs. Kroll sat at the table, the introductions had been made, and the mayor had explained the situation to her.

"So you see, madam, our dilemma," the mayor said.

"There is no dilemma to me," she said. "I understand you brought my husband here from out-of-state?"

The council, as a group, looked across the table to the Sheriff.

"You have no evidence," she said. "And I can prove absolutely that my husband and I have never, up until now, ever been in California - - let alone your town."

She paused, not to gain confidence - - she had enough of that - - but for effect.

"Is this how you administer the law in Campbell Station, gentlemen?"

The men were beaten and they knew it.

The mayor stood up. "Thank you, Mrs. Kroll," he said. "If you would excuse us for a minute, I'm sure we can bring this unfortunate matter to a satisfactory conclusion."

Mrs. Kroll was escorted from the room and when

the door had closed behind her the mayor addressed the council. "We have no alternative," he said. "We have to let him go - - agreed?"

It was a rhetorical question. Deputy Ayer brought Eli Kroll up from the cells and when he saw his wife he rushed to hold her.

Word swept through the town and those who had put their mark for the man were smug and satisfied, the others, some of them, embarrassed. There were a few, though, who felt cheated. This had seemed an end to the long, horrific affair but suddenly retribution was being denied again.

When Father O'Reilly heard the news he was relieved.

Trace went to the railroad station.

It was a different crowd that gathered there. Fewer than before, and mostly those who had opted for, not against, the man. The Sheriff had sent his deputies to see the Krolls onto the train; it was not a duty he felt inclined to do himself. In fact, when they had left the courthouse he had turned to the mayor and said, "This is not the end of it, Mr. Mayor. I'm not giving up here."

Eli and Caroline Kroll were smiling and talking to Torsen as the train pulled in. Torsen had wanted to tell them both how he had felt - - he didn't want Eli Kroll leaving without knowing that.

The train came to a standstill and as Caroline was helped up into the carriage by her husband, Trace stepped forward.

"Mr. Kroll," he said.

The Campbell Depot

Eli Kroll turned. "Yes, sir," he said. He seemed suddenly nervous.

"I wanted you to know I didn't put my name in that book."

"Oh, yes, I saw," Eli said. He turned, hesitated and looked back again to Trace. "I deeply appreciated that," he said.

"Really?" Trace said. "Hardly a vote of confidence, though. Sitting on the fence."

The man smiled. He put out his hand. "Thank you, nevertheless."

Trace moved closer to take the hand and shake it. He held on to the man's hand. His voice was low.

"Good-bye, Mr. . . . . . Kroll, have a safe journey." He paused and looked along the platform to the engine of the train. "Beats wheeling, at our time of life I would say."

One other passenger boarded that train, but there was no one to see him off.

Eli Kroll and his wife relaxed in their carriage. He leaned across and took his wife's hand.

"I owe you a lot for coming," he said.

"No. No, you don't," she said. "Why don't you try and sleep? There's some time before they serve dinner."

The man leaned back and closed his eyes and the soft swaying of the train and the rhythm of the wheels over the tracks gently lulled him. Images flitted through his mind and he could see flickers of flame in a dark night.

❧ ❧ ❧

It was the only house around there, outside of that small town in Nebraska. Spring had come early, but the night air was cold, and at first sight the flames looked comforting. He was trying for a safe place to stay, riding his bicycle and always trying for some safe place.

Then he heard the screams.

He pushed down on the pedals and rode hard over the dirt track that led up to the house that was burning. He could see the flames inside the house, curling up at the drapes at the windows, devouring them. The screams were coming from inside the house, a woman's screams. "Eli, Eli." Desperate panic in her voice.

The man threw the bicycle down and ran to the front door. As he crashed it open, the rush of air fanned the flames and they crossed the floor towards him like a furling yellow and red carpet. He could see the woman: she was crawling along the floor just inside the door of a bedroom. A cinder fell on her nightgown and it started to smolder into tiny licks of flame.

The man tried to shield his face from the heat, then his hands were on the woman, dragging her from the room. He lifted her and she screamed out again, "Eli, Eli."

He carried her across the hallway and when he got outside he took his coat off and threw it over her to put

192

out the flames that were burning at her nightgown.

She was choking and limp from the smoke, and her eyes, when she looked up at him, were wide with pleading as she tried to point to the house. The man left her there on the ground and he staggered back to the house. He thought he heard the sound of horses coming as he went through the door, then there was only the roaring of the fire. A dark shape in a room, a man leaning over a cot, the fire everywhere, another cot next to it. All of a sudden it was unreal, like he was in a hellish cauldron and everything around him was melting. The crackling of wood, and the crash, as burning beams fell.

The dark shape in front of him was burning, and as it fell backwards, the white face opened, but no sound came as the flames ate at the shape and the bundle he was holding in his arms. Then it was over and they were gone.

The man could feel the fire on himself, but he didn't seem to care; it was like he was reliving a nightmare. He reached into the second cot and pulled out a child, covered its tiny face and body with a blanket.

As he got to the door, there were people throwing buckets of water over him, and they took the child from him and gave it to its mother and they dragged him away from the house that was now a fiery mass collapsing onto the ground.

When he came to, the gray dawn was giving light to the charred wreck that was all that remained of the house. It looked to him like a black and white charcoal drawing; sticks poking into the sky at odd angles, and the smell of burnt lumber everywhere in the air.

There were people all around now, sifting through the still hot timbers that gave off a gray-blue smoke. Ash being spread over the earth by a soft, cool breeze. Dark figures moving slowly and treading carefully, no conversation, just the occasional voice.

"Nothing here."

"Everything's gone."

As he leaned up, an old woman with a cannister of cold water pressed it to his lips. "Drink this," she said.

The others saw him and they came over to the figure of him there on the ground drinking the water. He was a sorry looking sight. His hair and beard were singed short and his face and hands were black from the fire. His clothes were burnt and hung on him in shreds.

There was a mumuring from the people.

"How's he doin'?"

"A miracle he got out alive."

"Anyone know him?"

Disembodied voices to the man on the ground, coming from dark shapes standing over him.

He could feel spots of rain, falling without any rhythm and then gaining in speed until there was a pattering to them. He opened his eyes full and he saw the people clearly and what was left of the house. Then the rain was coming swift and hard but the people stayed put, not that there was any cover that he could see for them to run to if they wanted.

Water was soaking them all and he could feel it running down his face and when he went to wipe his eyes his hand came away with black ash on it. He could see the rain washing him clean of the ash, puddles of blackness on the ground.

As suddenly as it started the rain stopped even though the sky was gray without the slightest sight of blue anywhere.

A woman came to kneel by him. She looked drained and exhausted and she clutched a shawl around her shoulders. He recognized her. She was the woman he had dragged from the blazing house.

He opened his lips to speak, "How's the child?" The words came in rasps.

"She's alive, thanks to you."

The man tried to smile. "I have a boy myself," he said.

A farming man came to stand by them, then another, then there was a group around him.

"How is he?" one of the men said.

"You came through the fire all right," the farming man said.

"Takes some an' cleanses some," another said.

"Took nearly everything I ever had," the woman said.

The man on the ground tried to reach up to touch the woman as if he would comfort her.

❦ ❦ ❦

George Dougan thought there would be no end to it until they were all dead and gone and even then the legend would live after. He remembered traveling part way to St. Louis with John junior to the meeting that would be the last one between his brother and himself.

There was head hanging that day but no explanations because how does a man explain such things? He didn't talk about it either. It was something over and done with whatever he might think about it and he wasn't the sort to turn against his own brother even if he was of a very different mind. In any event he had his own life. His woman had a superstition and had said she could well do without the blood kin of John Dougan in her family; although she wasn't that superstitious that she turned away the money that had come with the boy. So, John getting himself fixed and a long ways from California worked out fine for all.

That was the end of it for him except on those days when he would think back to the times with John. They were memories for smiling before life turned around. Up at Chico, then at the house with Jane in San Jose. What can a man do about his future, he thought? You come to a crossway and who's to know which road and what might have been if you'd taken the other. You just go through it and at the end wonder why it didn't turn out the way you imagined.

Caroline came back to the compartment and she looked down at the sleeping figure. Well, it had been worth it, she thought. Coming all that way to upset the apple cart for those people in Campbell Station. Now it was all over and they could go back to living the life they had created for themselves a long time ago. Created it out of the ashes.

She leaned down and shook his shoulder.

"Eli, Eli. Come on, time to wake."

He opened his eyes and stretched and blinked in the soft light of the railroad carriage.

"Ah. That feels better," he said and he wondered where the fleeting images of sleep had gone.

They walked to the dining carriage, and over their dinner they were quiet, just passing the time of day like a regular married couple. The train was traveling slowly as it approached its climb to the Sierra Nevada.

A face suddenly appeared at the window of the door leading into the dining car, as if a person were glancing in to see if dinner was still being served.

Had Eli Kroll looked up he would have caught sight of eyes that were studying him. When he did turn his head, to look at the waiter standing at their table, the face had gone.

"How you folks doin'?" the waiter said.

"Just fine, thank you," Eli Kroll said.

"Lovely sight out there," the waiter said. "Startin' to snow again."

"Must be cold," Caroline said..

"Sure is. A person wouldn't last long on a night

197

like this." The waiter was pouring the wine while he was making conversation. "Freeze to death in no time. Then the bears'd get 'em."

"Oh." Caroline put her hand to her mouth. "My, you're right," she said. "With all that beauty I'd forgotten the danger lurking for a body out there alone.

"How we doing for time?" Eli said.

"Oh, fine, sir," the waiter said. "We got us a Malle Steam Engine. That's a wonderful piece of machinery. Why, we'll be doin' well up to sixty-nine miles per hour once over the mountains, sir."

"As much as that?"

"Sure thing lady. You know the record from Los Angles to Chicago is only a little over thirty hours. That's goin' some."

"Progress," Eli said.

"Sure enough," the waiter said.

"Shall we have a brandy do you think?" Eli said.

"Why not," Caroline said. "We've something to celebrate I suppose."

The waiter brought the brandies and some black coffee and the two of them sat there not talking, just looking out of the window or at other passengers in the dining car.

"Good health," Eli raised his glass.

"And yours," Caroline said.

"I'll be glad to get back to the children," Eli said.

"They missed you. Particularly John."

"There's no distinction between them," he reached across the table and gently squeezed Caroline's hand.

"We're a family, always will be."

They used to travel together a lot in the early years, she thought. First Iowa, then Indiana. It was in Indiana that he suggested making it legal, changing names. Strange how you accept things. How circumstances at the time give you justifications. It would be a clean slate for him, he had said. A new start and who was to know, except his brother and they were real close. It was simple, they would be the Krolls. A good Catholic family.

They moved down to Missouri after that, Eli, Caroline and John and Katie Kroll.

Considering what they had been through it would have seemed strange to an outsider that they didn't talk about it. But, they were that kind of couple. They never had talked much, a lot of thinking and long silences.

They understood each other well though.

"You must be tired, Caroline," he said.

She smiled at him. "Yes, I am."

They finished their drinks and Eli took care of the bill and they walked down the swaying, half lit corridor together putting arms out to steady themselves as the train took the curves in the track.

Many of the sleeping berths had their curtains pulled over, their occupants bedded down for the night. The clicky-clack of the train and its swaying in the dim light was hypnotic, particularly after a good dinner followed by a brandy and Eli Kroll could feel the heavy drowsiness.

A sleeping berth curtain, one on an upper deck,

shivered as they went by but they didn't notice the sharp eyes from behind it that watched them pass.

They got to their berth and Caroline sat on the edge of the lower one.

"I think I'll take a breath of fresh air before I turn in," Eli said.

"All right," Caroline said. "But take your top-coat." She smiled. "I brought it in case you needed it."

He bent down and kissed her on the cheek, "Good night my sweet dear. I'll try not to wake you when I get back."

"It wouldn't matter, Eli," she said.

❦ ❦ ❦

He stood huddled into his topcoat on the observation platform at the end of the train. It was snowing hard. He wouldn't stay out there too long, he thought. It was a beautiful night with the moonlight making black moving shadows as the train climbed through the Sierra Nevada. Strange to think it was over now, really over. Been close back there in Campbell, if she hadn't come he doubted he'd have got out alive. George would have been told of it by now and he would know they would probably never see each other again - - no more risks.

He drew on the cigar and the red end of it glowed in the cold night air. He thought about his boy, John.

He was going to be all right. Thirteen years old and at Catholic school, just as he had always wanted it. Bright boy too. He'd never tell him, the letter he had written along with his will would suffice when that time came.

He heard the door onto the platform open and he turned to see a shadowy figure standing there. "Good evening," he said. "It's fair cold out here."

The figure's voice came muffled through the thick scarf wrapped around the mouth, "Is it John Dougan?"

For some stange reason he knew it would be useless to deny it. "Yes," he said.

An awful sound, a deep drawn out cry, came from the figure.

John Dougan leaned as far back as he could against the railing of the observation platform.

The figure pulled his hand from the thick topcoat and there shone, in the clear icy moonlight, the clean shaft of a pointed blade.

"Hisler. You know that name?"

"I know it," John Dougan said.

Neither man made to move. It was as if they were there by design to wait out the final scene in a play that had been written and they were only players without any power to alter what was to be.

"Vengeance is mine. I will repay, saith the Lord. That's what the Book says, isn't it Dougan? I'm not waiting for anyone's Lord, yours or theirs. Some father in heaven, took a father on earth."

He struck, and the sharp edge of the knife cut into

John Dougan's throat.

Old man Hisler watched as the body slumped against the rail of the observation platform. The blood was already congealing in the freezing air. Just a thin red gash of an open throat. The snow was coming thicker, pure white flakes on the red throat.

He'd done it at last. Got back for what that Catholic swine had done to his daughter. He'd waited a long time for that. As far as he was concerned, it was their goddamn religions that had killed her as much as Dougan's axe.

He threw the knife out into the air. He must hurry before anyone else came out there.

The railroad tracks hugged one side of the mountain, the other fell sharply away, a drop of a thousand feet or more into the tree-covered gorges of the Sierra. He bent over and struggled to lift Dougan's legs and slowly the body toppled over the side of the safety rail. He saw it bounce on the tracks and then it went over into the darkness.

They'd never discover it there, he thought. If the animals didn't get it now it would freeze - - then in the spring they'd get it for sure. Maybe they'd find the bones some day. That had been a theory all the time, that the man had died in the mountains. Well, now he had.

Before he went back into the train to the bathroom, he checked the platform. The snow was washing the blood away. There was not much blood on himself - - surprising, really - - just on his hands and the front of his coat. When he had finished no one would ever notice.

He got off the train at Reno. It was still dark and nobody took any mind to an old man in the line of passengers leaving the station. Then he was gone.

Caroline Kroll woke as the train pulled out of Winnemucca. She saw immediately that Eli's berth was empty. The instant panic she felt faded when she saw the brown leather bag on the rack. He's gone to the dining car, she thought, for an early breakfast.

He always was an early riser.

She took her time dressing, and then she went along the corridor to the dining car. It was closed.

The panic returned. Where was he? What had happened? She started to go down the length of the train. As she walked along the center aisles of the Pullman cars she wanted to pull back the curtains of each sleeping compartment. But the reception she got the first time she did that persuaded her not to repeat it. Instead she checked with each car porter who went down his list of numbered berths. It took her over an hour to convince herself that Eli was no longer on the train.

She sat in the observation car and looked back along the tracks. In the far distance she could see the tips of the mountains. There had been two stops, she knew, since she had kissed him good night: Reno and Winnemucca, Nevada. He could have got off at either and she would never know. But why? Why leave now?

When the train arrived at St. Louis she took Eli's bag with her. There was nothing of value in it; she had looked. Just a change of shirt and underwear and his shaving things. Nothing a man would bother about leaving behind if he had a mind to.

So, she went back to her home and to the two children. She made excuses to them, that their father had been delayed - - then had to stay over for his work. As the days made weeks she ran out of plausible reasons. She called George Dougan on the telephone, but of course, he could tell her nothing.

In the end she told them a story that was as close to the truth as she could get without actually divulging the whole of it, or at least what she herself knew. Their father had stayed over with old friends, she said, and then gone on a wheeling expedition into the mountains. With tears in her eyes she told them she feared for him; that some catastrophe had occurred.

They cried together and they prayed that he would be safe and would return.

It was ironic that the one man who could have given the truth of it, had he chosen, old man Hisler, died only a week after returning to Campbell Station. He fell from his horse and broke his neck. He had been a fine horseman, in spite of his age, and people wondered how such an accident could occur.

Some men, it is said, come to a point in their lives where there is nothing left for them to accomplish, or so they think. It is then, when the will leaves them, that strange accidents or maladies take them.

In the spring of the next year, when the snow melted in the Sierra Nevada and filled Lake Tahoe and the Truckee River and the hundreds of streams and tributaries that flowed into the valleys, a party of mountain hikers discovered the bones of a man. Only remnants of his clothes remained and there was nothing that could identify what was left of the corpse. The find was eventually reported to the authorities as yet another possibility of the Dougan remains. There had been many such reports over the years.

In a small town in Missouri the two children grew into adulthood. Then they went away to college, and on balmy summer days Caroline would sit on the porch of her house and she would recall the times of them together and there was always one memory that was so much clearer than all the others.

It was hot that day and John was out on the narrow roadway outside the house with the children and the new bicycle. She stood by the gate watching them. The grass alongside the road had grown long and there were butterflies going from one beautiful wild flower to the next and there were bees in the air; if you were quiet enough you could hear the sounds of the day. She was wearing a green floral dress, she remembered.

Katie was laughing so hard she was doubled over and John junior was trying to be serious because his father was explaining the ways of bicycling and they all knew that was a very serious subject. This was not his first time on a bicycle but his father was very strict about the proper techniques.

"It's your turn, John," he said and he helped his son mount the bicycle. "Now go straight and true."

The pedals had been adjusted so that the boy's feet could touch them at their furthest extension. John Dougan held him from the back and then with a push he was off down the lane weaving and touching the tall grass as he went from side to side.

"That's it, John, keep the pedals turning and you'll straighten up as you go."

They were full of fun, then they heard the sound of the bakery van.

John junior had a steam up and he was riding without hands and the van was coming and Caroline had tensed up and she was clutching the tops of her arms with hands folded across her chest.

She turned to John and his body was poised and the feet well spread and he was leaning forward his eyes on his son's back. As the van rounded the corner she saw John Dougan's hips swivel as if it were himself on the bicycle and was to make a turn. Instinct, it seemed, took over John junior and his command of the bicycle as he made a change of direction. He waved at Joseph the baker as they passed each other on that narrow lane. She relaxed then and John was turning in the lane and coming back to them.

"Mornin' Caroline, Eli." The baker leaned from the van.

"Good morning, Joseph," they said.

"Sure is a fine boy there, Eli." He took a deep breath, "An' some hand with a bicycle."

"Yeah," Dougan said and there was the pride of reflected glory in his voice. "Growing up right, that's all you can want - - for 'em to grow up right."

Caroline had never forgotton that phrase of John's, "Growing up right." It was an obsession with him that his son would grow to be a good Catholic, as if that would be justification for his own sins. He was a wounded soul John Dougan was.

She had kept the letter he had written for John junior. Kept it safe at his request to give to the boy when he reached twenty-one, if he weren't there to do it himself. Many times she had been tempted to open it. To know what he had said to his son about his real mother and the terrible time that had changed their world.

She died without reading it though and it passed to its rightful addressee intact.

THE LEGEND OF JOHN DOUGAN

EPILOGUE

THE LEGEND OF JOHN DOUGAN

EPILOGUE

Oak Hill Cemetery, San Jose, California, 1960.

The thick-set man read each gravestone carefully, one after the other:

Joseph Daniels
Born: July 13, 1866
Died: May 26, 1896
VENGEANCE

Col. Alexander McDonald
Born: May 21, 1841
Died: May 26, 1896
IS MINE

Daisy Hanson
Born: September 15, 1842
Died: May 26, 1896
I WILL REPAY

Cathy Hanson
Daughter of John Harold and Daisy Hanson
Born: December 11, 1869
Died: May 26, 1896
SAITH

Samuel Hanson
Born: July 6, 1873
Died: May 26 1896
THE LORD

He walked away from the graves then and back towards the rented automobile that he had parked in the narrow roadway.

The ground was soft from the continuous rain, and the grayness of the graves and flying angels that were frozen into stone made it a dreary place.

They had large and seemingly fragile families in those days, the man thought. Many of the small, upright stones had just the word Baby carved into them. Tears long ago shed.

He drove the car back up the inner road of the cemetery to the office building and parked again. Inside the reception lobby the nicely dressed, quiet woman looked up as he walked across the thick pile carpet towards her desk. The lighting was discreet and muted.

"Did you find what you wanted, Father?" she said. Her voice was low and reverential.

The priest wiped the rainwater from his face with a handkerchief. He smiled at the woman.

"Wet day," he said.

"Yes," the woman said. "Keeps most people at home, a day like this. Would you like our booklet on the history of Oak Hill? We have some very famous people here, you know. Some from the Donner Pass party."

"No, I don't think so, thank you," the priest said. "I won't be coming back."

"Oh."

"I just wanted to thank you for your help."

"Yes, you're very welcome. Not many come to see the Hanson plot anymore. You noticed the inscription?"

"Yes," the priest said. "I know the exact quotation of course." His voice was even and soft. "Dearly beloved, avenge not yourselves, but rather give place unto wrath: for it is written, Vengeance is mine; I will repay, saith the Lord."

He paused. "Romans 12:19."

The woman was impressed and a little uneasy. "Well now, that is absolutely correct," she said. "They never did get him, the husband, though. Not even a body."

The priest smiled. "Nor did they allow his name where it belonged, on his wife's gravestone." he said.

"Oh, that's right, yes you're right," the woman said. "Cathy Dougan, not Cathy Hanson."

She sighed and looked down at a black presentation book on the desk top in front of her.

"Would you like to sign our visitor's book before you leave?" she said.

"Yes, of course," the priest said.

She opened the lined book with its names and addresses from across the United States and beyond even, and she handed the priest a pen to use.

He took the pen, and in a careful and neat hand wrote his name. He did not write in an address, just a state.

"Did you ever wonder," he said, "whether the Lord took his revenge?"

The woman didn't at first grasp what the priest had said. Then she turned the visitor's book around, so that she could read the signature. The expression on her face was at first one of mystification.

The priest was buttoning his Burberry topcoat, and as he turned to leave, he smiled at the woman.

"Thank you again for your help," he said.

"You're welcome, Father," the woman said, but she was not really paying attention.

The priest walked away from her across the peach colored carpet and out of the door into the pouring rain. She lifted the spectacles that were dangling from a jeweled chain around her neck and she studied the last signature in the book.

The writing was very clear:

> John Dougan, Jr.
> Bishop of All Angel's
> Missouri

AND SO THE LEGEND BEGAN

THE LEGEND OF JOHN DOUGAN

This story is true insofar as the real John Dougan's marriage, acts of murder, escape, return to Campbell, and subsequent lack of evidence to hold in custody are concerned. He was never captured and the stories of where he went, what he did and how he ended up are endless.

I had some correspondence with a former columnist of the *San Jose Mercury News*, Dick Barrett, who added his contribution in the form of steering me in the direction of a gentleman named Sherman Millard.

Sherman's father was a journalist back in the time of the murders and had acquired photographs of the dead together with a copy of the original "Wanted Dead or Alive" poster.

I therefore owe Mr. Millard not only a debt of thanks for his permission to use and reproduce the material, but for both his and his wife's kind hospitality. The photographs have been used on the front and back cover and on pages 68, 135, 136, 137, 138, 152, and 157.

In addition, I want to express my thanks to Jeanette Watson, the former Mayor of Campbell, Peggy Coats and Jean-Anne Marshall-Clark of the Campbell Museum, and Kevin Duggan, the Campbell City Manager, for their generous cooperation.

I am happy to acknowledge the City of Campbell, the Historical Resources Supervisor, and the Museum Board for permission to reproduce the photographs on pages 33, 34, 35, 71, 154, and 190.

I should also state that the Campbell Historical

Museum takes no responsibility for the historical accuracy of this work.

Finally, my thanks to the California State Library for their permission to reproduce the illustrations on pages 28, 83, 123, 130, 132, 146, 149, 154, and 167. Incidentally, these were manufactured from projection prints taken from actual pages of the *San Jose Mercury News*. It would be lax of me not to thank Kathleen C. Eustis, the librarian, and her staff, for their generous assistance; I am very pleased to do that here.

In the process of creating the novel I changed the names of some of the major characters to protect any living relatives. As it happened I did, only recently, talk to a close relative of the murderer's great grandson.

I created all the story beyond the recorded facts based on my assumptions of the evidence I studied, and a writer's typical penchant for dramatic invention.

I read that the American Protective Association ceased to exist in 1911. As far as is currently known this secret society has never been reactivated.

Robert Pollock
Walnut Creek, California.
March 1991